# THE SHADOW OF ATLANTIS

## Wendy Leighton-Porter

Written in English (UK)

ISBN 978-1-4710-8899-5

Published by Mauve Square Publishing

2012

www.mauvesquare.com

For Simon,
thank you for your unfailing love, support and
encouragement.

And for Mum,
who always told me I could do it!

# Prologue

In a state of total panic and scarcely able to believe the sight which met his eyes, Max hadn't a clue what he should do. A strange cloud, glowing with a mysterious inner light, filled the middle of the room and through the mist he saw what seemed to be the shadowy image of an ancient city. It was rather like the mirage of an oasis floating before the eyes of a traveller in a desert and, in the same way that a mirage seems real, but shimmers in the heat haze before gradually fading from view, so the fuzzy outline of the town flickered and began to disappear.

Suddenly a hand reached out through the mist, clawing desperately at the bare floorboards of the attic as though trying to grab hold of something, while faint, panic-stricken voices cried out from within the cloud.

'Where's the key?'

'I don't know. I can't find the wretched thing. I must

have left it on the floor next to the book.'

'But we're stuck without the key, Isabel. We won't be able to get back.'

'Oh my God, what are we going to do?'

Eventually the anguished cries grew fainter as the image of the city continued to fade and the searching hand withdrew from sight. Then all was quiet once more.

Max cocked his head on one side and focused his aquamarine eyes on the last shreds of mist, but there was no longer any sign of the outstretched arm. The desperate voices had ceased and only the rasping of his own breath broke the silence as he gasped in horror. Alone and afraid, he remained rooted to the spot and rubbed a paw over his eyes, staring at the empty space where the vision had been. He settled down to wait for them to come back, but the gateway to the past had now closed and they'd vanished.

In the middle of the floor a carved wooden chest, its open lid revealing a threadbare blue velvet lining, sat beside an old book whose leather cover bore an intricate design. Next to the book and the chest lay Isabel's favourite gold necklace on which hung an unusual charm. It was the only evidence of the weird event which had just taken place.

# Chapter 1

The policeman gazed around the room with a perplexed frown. 'Well, sir, I must say this is all a bit odd. I can't see any sign of a struggle in the house, nothing's been broken, there isn't anything missing and the front door was locked. I'm sure they'll turn up safe and sound - that's what often happens, in my experience. There'll be a simple explanation, you mark my words.'

'Officer, my brother and his wife wouldn't just disappear, abandoning their children,' said Richard Lancelot. 'And besides, their car is still on the drive so they can't have gone far, but they've been missing for over twenty-four hours now. What on earth can have happened to them?'

The policeman shrugged and shook his head, having no answer to this question. Tired and worried, Richard Lancelot pushed his floppy, light-brown fringe out of his eyes and looked around the attic in complete bewilderment. The only clues they'd found were two sets of footprints on the dusty floorboards, which stopped abruptly in the middle of the room, and also a piece of gold jewellery belonging to Isabel.

'She always wore this,' mused Richard. 'She wouldn't have gone anywhere without it.' He picked up the necklace, inspecting it closely. The clasp didn't appear to be broken, so it seemed unlikely that the chain had simply fallen off. James and Isabel had apparently vanished into thin air and Richard had no idea what had become of them. The real problem for now was the twins. What would happen to them if their parents didn't return?

******

**3 months later**

The rain lashed at Jemima's bedroom window and she watched in misery as the drops turned into rivulets which trickled relentlessly down the panes of glass. For the past few weeks she'd gazed at the sun-dappled playground outside the classroom, counting the days until the end of term. She'd struggled to settle at their new school and had missed her old friends from home. Now the dismal weather this morning, the first day of the summer holidays, reminded her of her sadness and she burrowed her nose into the comforting fur of the sleeping heap by her side. At once a loud rumbling purr started up and Jemima snuggled closer to the big cat lying next to her. She'd just begun to doze off again when she was awoken by an almighty yell as her bedroom door burst open with a crash.

'Come on, Jem. Time to get up, Lazy Bones.' Jemima's twin brother Joe exploded into the room, causing the startled cat to leap from the bed and dash out through the door, complaining as he went. Jemima also grumbled and attempted to bury herself under the duvet, but Joe proved too quick for her and snatched the cover off the bed.

'We're on holiday, Jem. Don't waste time lying around in bed all day.'

She glanced at her watch. Nine o'clock. Huh! Hardly all day. Did he always have to be so noisy and full of energy? Reluctantly, she crawled out of bed and followed Joe downstairs.

Mrs Garland, Uncle Richard's housekeeper who came in every day to clean and cook, was bustling around the kitchen. 'Hello, my loves. Sit yourselves down. Breakfast will be ready in two shakes of a lamb's tail.' Joe caught Jemima's eye and they grinned at each other - she did say some funny things. Mrs Garland, a large, jolly lady with a kind and gentle nature, had developed a soft spot for the ten-year-old twins since they'd come to live at their uncle's house and she clucked round them like a mother hen. In fact she reminded

5

Jemima of a character from a Beatrix Potter story, providing a warm and comforting presence in the house when Uncle Richard was out.

Their uncle, a professor of archaeology at the University of London, wasn't married, being far too wrapped up in his work and even spending most of his holidays on some archaeological dig or other. As a result he had little experience of dealing with children, although he loved his niece and nephew dearly. Being more accustomed to retiring to his study, surrounded by dry, dusty books, pieces of broken pottery and bits of ancient bones, he was still getting used to having the sounds of youngsters around the house.

Jemima was also finding it hard to adjust to her new life. She missed her parents awfully and, although Joe did his best to stay cheerful, she knew he did too. She was lucky they both got on so well – perhaps because they were twins. Some of her friends' brothers did horrible things to *them* like putting earwigs in their breakfast cereals or sticking chewing gum in their hair.

As for her mum and dad, Jemima thought about them all the time. They still didn't know what had happened to them and, although the police had conducted a nationwide hunt and their disappearance had been all over the news, the mystery remained unsolved. Of course, everyone feared the worst. Sometimes, however, Jemima felt her parents weren't far away and that they were watching over the two of them. She even convinced herself that her mother spoke to her at times and Isabel's voice sounded so real Jemima expected to find her standing in the room. Joe told her it was just wishful thinking, but she wasn't so sure.

At first, coming to live with Uncle Richard had been a huge shock for the twins as it had meant leaving their family home in Gloucestershire and they'd found moving into his rambling Victorian house in South London an awful wrench.

'You can each have a big bedroom,' Uncle Richard had said kindly, trying to make it easier for the twins. 'I'll even get them decorated however you choose. And, of course, don't forget Max can come too.' Although this meant that Jemima worried constantly about Max now they lived on a busy main road. He wasn't a city cat at all, being more used to the quiet country lanes and fields where they'd lived before.

No ordinary cat, Max was enormous - not fat, just extremely large - and they'd named him Max, short for Maximus, because of his spectacular size. Whenever he went to the vet, other people in the waiting room would gape in amazement when they peered into his basket, saying things like, 'What on earth have you got in there? Is it a mountain lion?' or 'Hasn't he got a long snout? He looks more like a hound than a cat.'

Even the vet himself admired him. 'Aren't you a handsome boy, Max? What a noble profile you've got!' he used to say. Max thought the vet's flattery was just to soften him up before inflicting some terrible indignity on him, such as inserting a thermometer up his rear end or jabbing a needle into the back of his neck, but it was true; he was indeed an extremely aristocratic-looking animal.

In fact Max happened to be a Tonkinese cat, a breed which had first been created by crossing a Siamese with a Burmese. On the day they chose him from a litter of six adorable, furry bundles, the breeder informed the family his official colour was "lilac".

'We've got a lilac kitten,' Jemima proudly told her friends when she next saw them.

'A purple cat? Don't be silly, Jemima,' they'd laughed and she got quite cross with them all for not understanding. She thought Max the most gorgeous creature she'd ever seen, with his creamy-coloured coat and the pale mushroomy-grey fur on his ears, muzzle, paws and tail. His lovely aquamarine eyes accentuated his beauty even further.

Jemima adored him from day one and, in return, Max followed Jemima everywhere like a puppy. He didn't miaow in the way ordinary cats do. Instead he made such a variety of different sounds that he almost sounded human at times.

'I think that cat would talk to us if he could, you know,' her mum often used to say. He certainly seemed to understand everything they said to him and he even smiled, according to Jemima who swore his mouth turned up at the corners when he was happy.

Breakfast over, Jemima and Joe helped Mrs Garland clear the kitchen table after they'd finished eating.

'So, what are you two planning to do with yourselves this morning?' she asked. 'Your uncle has got lectures today, but he said he'll try and get home early so you can all plan a day out together for tomorrow. Maybe you can think up a few ideas of what you'd like to do.'

'All right, Mrs G,' answered Joe. 'And Charlie's coming over to play, if that's okay.'

'Of course, my love. You go on up and get yourselves ready,' she replied, as she turned to start loading the dishwasher.

Charlie Green lived next door and, being the same age as Joe and Jemima, had been delighted when they'd moved in, soon becoming firm friends with Joe. Charlie had never had a close friend before. Small for his age, brown-haired and with big round glasses, he'd often found himself the butt of other children's teasing: some of them called him names like "Geek" or "Four Eyes" or even "Harry Potter". Now, he had Joe at his side, school was much more enjoyable. As Joe quickly became a popular member of the class, thanks to his friendship, Charlie also began to be included in everything, delighted to be accepted by the other children at long last.

He'd already known the story about Joe and Jemima's parents from the news on the TV. His mum, Ellen, had also explained what had happened.

'You can help them settle in, Charlie,' she told him after the twins' uncle had sought her advice. 'They're going to need a friend when they move down here and they don't know anybody.'

Charlie also thought he understood a little bit of what they might be going through. Since his own parents' divorce, Charlie missed having his dad at home, but at least he still got to spend most weekends with him. He realised how much worse things must be for Joe and Jemima knowing they might never see either of their parents again.

# Chapter 2

The doorbell rang as Jemima was tying her long blonde hair into a ponytail. She heard Joe whoop as he hurtled down the stairs to let Charlie in and the next instant two pairs of thundering feet charged back upstairs again and along to Joe's bedroom. Jemima was just starting to feel a little left out when her door opened and Joe stuck his head round.

'Are you ready, Jem? We're going upstairs to find that book of Mum and Dad's. Uncle Richard said we're allowed as long as we're careful. Coming?'

She nodded and went out on to the landing to join them. 'Hi, Charlie,' she said.

'Hi.' He gave her a shy smile.

They both followed Joe up the staircase to the spare room on the top floor, where their parents' things were being stored while Uncle Richard tried to decide what to do with the family house in Gloucestershire. Joe opened the door and all three of them trooped inside. Both twins experienced a sudden pang of sadness when confronted by

11

their mum and dad's belongings, but Joe marched over to a shelf on the far side of the room and lifted down a heavy wooden box which he placed carefully on the floor.

The spare room was a bit gloomy because the windows were much smaller than downstairs, so they knelt on the carpet to get a closer look. As Joe began to blow the dust off the top of the box an eerie grating noise made them jump and the door to the room started to open all by itself. They turned round, staring fearfully at the door as it swung inwards with a sinister creak. Holding their breath, the three children cast anxious glances at one another, but then a long, mushroom-coloured muzzle appeared and a pair of pale turquoise eyes peeped around the half-opened door.

'Oh Max, you frightened us,' laughed Jemima, as he trotted over to her with a chirrup.

The relieved children returned their attention to the wooden chest on the floor between them. Ornately carved, it looked terribly old to them and as Joe began to lift the lid, a musty odour rose up causing Max to wrinkle his nose and sneeze several times. Inside lay an ancient book, its leather cover decorated with a complicated swirly pattern.

At first glance it didn't seem terribly exciting, and the twins wondered why this had been one of their parents' most treasured possessions. They'd kept the chest in the attic and had spent many hours studying the book, saying they mustn't be disturbed. To tell the truth, Jemima felt rather disappointed now seeing the old book sitting in its box. She'd expected something much more thrilling. Her father, who'd been a dealer in second-hand books, had travelled all over the world seeking rare editions of ancient texts and had been beside himself when he'd found this particular one. Just what was so special about it? It looked rather shabby in her opinion.

'Let's get it out so we can have a proper look,' said Joe. He gingerly slid his hands underneath and lifted the book out, placing it on the floor with a thump. 'Phew, that's heavy.' However, when he attempted to open it, the cover simply wouldn't budge. 'Impossible,' he puffed. 'You have a go, Charlie.'

Charlie gripped the edges of the cover and tried his hardest to lift it up, but nothing happened. 'I can't. It seems to be stuck down.'

'I know,' suggested Joe. 'I'll go and fetch a knife from the kitchen and we'll prise it open.'

'No,' squeaked Jemima, horrified. 'Don't be stupid. Remember what Uncle Richard said. We mustn't damage it or we'll be in big trouble.'

They studied the cracked leather binding on which was

13

inscribed the title: *SHADOWS FROM THE PAST.*

'Hmm, that sounds interesting,' said Charlie. 'I wonder what it's about.'

Max moved closer, patting the cover with an exploratory paw.

'No, Max, don't touch,' scolded Jemima and pulled him away.

Joe began to trace his fingers over the gilded pattern on the cover. 'Hold on, what's this?' he exclaimed. Under his fingertip he'd detected a small hole, concealed within the intricate design.

'It's like a keyhole,' said Charlie. 'Just our luck though – there's no key.'

At that moment Jemima let out a yelp causing Joe and Charlie to leap back from the book in surprise. 'Yes there is,' she said. 'I think I might be wearing it. Ouch, it's hot.'

'Don't talk rubbish,' replied Joe. 'What's hot?'

'After Mum and Dad disappeared Uncle Richard found this gold chain. He said it was Mum's and he gave it to me. I like wearing it to remind me of her.' As Jemima spoke, something weird began to happen. The charm hanging on the necklace had now become unbearably hot and had started to really burn her skin, so she reached inside her tee shirt and pulled it away from her neck. Joe and Charlie,

14

who'd already been a little startled by Jemima's cry, now both let out a gasp as they stared at the strangely-shaped charm. It may have been a trick of the light but it seemed to be glowing.

'Take it off, Jem,' urged her brother.

'Okay, but do be careful with it.' She unhooked the clasp and handed him the necklace. Joe took it from her, holding the chain up so that all three of them could see it properly. Now there was no doubt: the charm was definitely giving off a bright light.

Charlie peered at it intently. 'That's the key all right.' He pointed to the charm. 'Look at the shape of it. It's like a number 8 and that's what this keyhole thingy feels like too.'

Joe leaned over and placed the necklace above the hole. 'I think you could be right, Charlie.' As he pushed downwards the charm instantly slotted into place with a quiet click and at once the whole book seemed to tremble beneath his hands. Max took a few steps back, his fur standing on end, making him appear even bigger than usual, but the children were far too engrossed to notice.

'Right,' said Joe. 'I wonder if it'll open now.' Together they all took hold of the cover and this time there was no resistance. As it opened a small sigh escaped from within the depths of the book and the children heard what sounded like faint whispering voices, but couldn't make them out clearly.

'I'm not sure about this. It's a bit scary,' murmured Jemima, her voice starting to quaver.

'Nonsense,' replied Joe. 'It's brilliant.' He turned to the opening chapter. The first page was beautiful; it looked like a medieval illuminated manuscript, written in italics, decorated in rich colours and embellished with gold leaf. The children gazed in wonder.

'Wow, that's really pretty. I can understand why Mum and Dad liked this book so much now,' breathed Jemima.

The title of the first chapter, however, was a strange word none of them recognised and which seemed to be written in tiny, jewelled stones. The sparkly gems spelled out:

### *TALISANT*

And underneath was printed the following rhyme:

*A fabled city lost to time, a distant place we can't recall.*
*Was it real or just a myth? Was it ever there at all?*
*The waters rose and cover'd the land, then everything*
*fell from sight.*
*The people perish'd, time stood still and all was endless*
*night.*

'How strange,' said Jemima. 'I wonder what it's about. I've never heard of "*Talisant*". Shall we see if it tells us on the next page?'

But when Joe tried to turn over the page nothing happened. The paper seemed to be glued down.

'Oh no, not again,' wailed Charlie.

'Well, I can't see another keyhole,' said Joe.

They hadn't noticed Max creeping closer to the book for a second time and, as they all sat back on their heels pondering their next move, he once more stretched out a paw as if to touch the page.

'Max!' shouted Jemima. 'I've already told you to leave it alone. If you don't behave I'll have to put you outside.' Max grumbled and slunk off to a corner of the room, sulking.

'Maybe the keyhole is really small this time and we're just not looking carefully enough,' suggested Jemima. The children all bent forward, staring at the page until they almost became cross-eyed. '...or maybe not,' she concluded after several minutes of intense concentration.

Joe trailed his fingers over the surface of the paper, feeling for anything their eyes may have missed, but on touching the sparkling letters he quickly withdrew his hand and sat back with a start.

'What's the matter?' asked Jemima, seeing the worried

expression on his face.

'I'm not sure, but I thought something moved. I don't want to spoil it and, if the stones aren't glued on properly, they might fall off. We'd get into awful trouble with Uncle Richard for ruining the book ... and, besides, it belonged to Mum and Dad,' he added quietly.

But as the three of them looked at the page they saw the jewelled letters starting to quiver. Jemima placed a trembling index finger on the first letter *T*. 'The whole thing moved,' she exclaimed in an excited whisper. 'But I don't think the stones are loose.' She ran her fingertip down the page a little and the *T* followed beneath her touch. 'That's weird. This still feels firmly attached to the paper, but it just slides about on the surface. I wonder why?' She began to try the same thing with the other letters in the title and, sure enough, they all moved in an identical manner.

'What on earth's going on?' asked Joe. The capital letters were now scattered all over the place and the word *TALISANT* had become *A TIN SLAT*. 'Let me try.' He moved everything around again until it spelled out *SNAIL TAT*.

Charlie had been watching thoughtfully. 'Perhaps this is a bit like one of those puzzles where you have to unjumble the word to find the answer. You know, they're called anagrams I think.' He had a go at sliding the letters around, but only managed to produce *ANT TAILS*.

'This is hopeless,' said Jemima. 'How can you possibly be expected to know what the real word is meant to be?'

They all had a think for a moment, staring at the page for inspiration.

'Maybe we've got to find another clue first,' suggested Charlie.

'Well, the only other thing I can see is the poem,' said Joe glumly.

Jemima's eyes suddenly lit up. 'That's it – the poem *is* the clue. I think it might be a sort of riddle and, if we work out the answer, that'll give us the missing word.' She began to read the rhyme out loud while the two boys listened, hoping to spot something important. From the corner of the room they could hear Max muttering and making odd noises, but kept telling him to shush because he was stopping them from concentrating.

Then Charlie had another of his brainwaves. 'Listen, we know this book is to do with things from a long time ago. After all it's called "*SHADOWS FROM THE PAST*" isn't it? The poem describes a myth about a city – a city destroyed by water, which disappeared for ever and where all the people died. Does that ring any bells?'

Joe shook his head, but Jemima's eyes opened wide as

she recalled where she'd heard something similar quite recently. 'Yes, it sounds like that story we read at school this term... and remember the film too... Is it **ATLANTIS**?'

Charlie nodded his agreement. 'I think so.'

Jemima started to rearrange the jewelled letters on the page. One at a time she moved them into the correct order and, as she slid the final *S* on to the end, something odd began to happen. The word suddenly lit up as if someone had flicked on a switch.

At once the children were surrounded by eerie sounds, accompanied by the distant lapping of waves on a sea shore and they all felt a gentle breeze which seemed to be blowing through the room. Then the pages of the book began to turn by themselves as if by magic. Wide-eyed in wonder, they started to read about the lost city of Atlantis, taking it in turns to recite the story aloud. With each passing page the sound of the waves grew louder and the breeze blew more strongly, ruffling their hair.

The children were too absorbed in the tale to notice what was going on behind them until all of a sudden Max gave an almighty yowl, making the three youngsters almost leap out of their skins. His fur was standing on end and, following his petrified gaze, they couldn't believe their eyes. For in the middle of the room had appeared a large shadow which seemed to be taking a more solid form the more they stared into its mysterious depths. Colours and shapes gradually began to emerge. It was like a film, but, instead of being projected against a white background, the image was floating in the air, making it seem semi-transparent. Nevertheless, the three children could see the three-dimensional vision of an ancient city forming before them and the whole thing seemed staggeringly real.

'C-c-crikey,' stammered Charlie. 'W-w-where's that coming from?'

Joe leapt to his feet and went over to the strange apparition. Cautiously he stretched out his arm and as he touched the mist his wrist disappeared inside. From the outside it looked as if his hand had been chopped off. Charlie and Jemima gasped in horror, but Joe merely said, 'Cool,' and immediately stuck his head into the cloud. He now appeared to be headless, but his voice drifted faintly back towards them sounding rather muffled, as if he was speaking from a long way away; the others couldn't understand a word he was saying.

All of a sudden Jemima became aware of someone calling to her in an urgent voice. 'Quick, Jemima, stop him.' *Funny, that sounds like Mum,* she thought. She scrambled to her feet and ran over to Joe. Grabbing him by his other arm she yanked him back so hard that he landed on his bottom with a crash.

'Oi, why did you do that? You'll never believe the things inside there,' he gabbled excitedly, pointing towards the mist. 'There's a beach and loads of people rushing about wearing weird clothes - you know, tunics and stuff like they wore thousands of years ago – and everyone's speaking some sort of foreign language. I haven't a clue what's going on, but this is brilliant!'

Charlie and Jemima stared at him in disbelief.

'It's true,' he insisted. 'Go on, have a look if you don't believe me.'

Charlie hesitantly approached the image and poked an experimental finger inside. At once his finger disappeared from view and, horrified, he snatched it straight back again.

'What's the matter? It didn't hurt, did it?' asked Joe.

'No-o-o,' replied Charlie, sounding a little unsure.

'Well, go on, have a proper look,' urged Joe. 'You'll be fine.'

So Charlie slowly leaned forward until his head had vanished from sight. After a few seconds he reappeared.

'He's right, Jemima. It's just like he said. You've got to see this.'

Jemima hung back. A horrible sensation of unease swept

over her and she suddenly felt terribly cold. The woman's voice sounded like her mother's, or was it just wishful thinking? 'No, don't,' it seemed to say. 'Not without the necklace, not without the necklace ....' Then it faded. She shivered and glanced across at the boys, but they didn't seem to have heard it so she said nothing.

While they were trying to persuade her to have a closer look, Max had emerged from the corner of the room where he'd been lurking and sidled up to the wooden chest which lay open on the floor. A scratching noise made Jemima turn round and, glancing back, she caught sight of what he was up to and gave a shriek of alarm. 'No, Max, bad cat!'

Max had found a loose piece of cotton in the worn fabric lining of the box and now his claws had somehow got tangled up in it. When Jemima yelled at him she watched in horror as he leapt backwards, pulling an ever-growing length of thread with him as the velvet began to unravel. 'Oh no,' she wailed, as she tried to grab hold of the retreating cat. 'Look, the fabric's ruined.'

'Wait a minute,' exclaimed Joe, as he came to inspect the damage. 'What's this under the material?' Beneath the hole Max had created they could clearly make out a compartment in the base of the box. 'Hey, I think there's something down here.' He probed with his fingers and extracted a small

23

pouch.

'What's inside?' asked Jemima, bursting with curiosity, her earlier fright now forgotten.

Joe felt hard edges through the soft leather and, untying the drawstring, he peered in. 'I can see something shiny - could be coins,' he said and tipped the contents into his other hand. No, it wasn't money. Instead, four gleaming objects lay in his palm. 'I don't know what these are, but they look as if they're made of gold.' Each one was identical.

'They look like the things that go on a charm bracelet,' said Jemima who picked them up in turn. 'They're little owls, how sweet. And look, they've got small rings on their heads so you can put them on a chain.'

'Yeah, but what are they for and why hide them in that compartment?' asked Charlie, as he picked one up between his thumb and forefinger, inspecting the golden charm at close range. It was exquisitely made and every detail of the bird's feathers was engraved with incredible precision.

'We'd better not lose them,' said Joe, tipping them back into the leather bag and carefully pulling the drawstring tight. 'We'll show these to Uncle Richard when he gets home. He might know.' For now Joe pushed the small pouch into the pocket of his jeans.

At that moment a voice called up the stairs. 'Are you

24

children all right? You've been rather quiet. Would you like a drink or something?'

'No thanks, Mrs Garland. We're fine. We're just reading a story in an old book,' replied Jemima.

Smiling, the housekeeper went back to the kitchen, relieved that they seemed to be occupying themselves so sensibly. No DVDs or footballs today – that made a pleasant change! She could go and get on with the ironing in peace.

As soon as she was out of earshot the children returned their attention to the image of the city which still shimmered brightly in the gloomy room.

'Why don't we all step inside and have a look round?' suggested Joe. 'It'll be a real adventure.'

'I'm not sure I want to,' said Jemima, recalling the voice and the sudden feeling of cold. 'Actually I'm quite frightened.'

'Don't be such a girl. What could possibly go wrong?' he replied. 'We'll have a look round and then come straight back. If we all stick together we'll be fine and just think what we'll be able to tell everyone afterwards.'

'Except they'll never believe us,' said Charlie. 'And anyway, Joe, are you sure we'll be able to get back again if we go in there?'

'Oh, that settles it,' said Jemima, folding her arms across

her chest, her mouth set in a stubborn line. 'I'm definitely not going – not if there's a chance of being stranded. You just don't think do you, Joe?'

'Watch me!' he exclaimed and, before either of them could stop him, he launched himself into the cloud. Max, however, had moved swiftly and sunk his teeth into the heel of Joe's trainer, clinging on for dear life and preventing him from disappearing entirely; one foot remained behind. Joe stepped backwards into the room, angrily shaking his shoe to free himself from the cat's jaws. 'Get off, you daft animal. What d'you think you're playing at?'

Max returned to Jemima's side, feeling rather pleased with himself and sporting a smug grin as he watched Joe inspect his trainer for teeth marks.

'Well, here I am back again, in one piece as you can see,' said Joe triumphantly. 'So there's obviously no problem coming and going, is there? You agree with me don't you, Charlie?'

'Hmm ... I s'pose.'

'See,' continued Joe, ignoring the note of doubt in Charlie's voice and clearly not prepared to take no for an answer. 'Even Charlie thinks it's safe. C'mon, Jem. Don't be wet.'

Jemima finally relented. 'Okay,' she said reluctantly.

Everything told her this wasn't a good idea, but she didn't want to be left behind on her own while the boys disappeared off to goodness knows where without her.

Joe went first, stepping confidently forward into the shimmering mist, closely followed by Charlie. In an instant they both vanished, which rather startled Jemima and as she hesitated she heard the same voice calling to her from far away – yet again it sounded just like her mum. 'Don't forget the necklace, Jemima. Pick up the necklace,' it urged.

Glancing down, Jemima realised the chain was still lying on the floor where they'd left it after using the charm to unlock the book. She scooped it up and, putting the necklace round her neck, made sure the clasp was securely fastened. As she did so she became aware of Joe's and Charlie's muffled voices. 'Come on, Jemima. Where are you?' Taking a deep breath she moved towards the shadowy image and with Max pushing against the back of her legs she stepped forwards, feeling the comforting pressure of his furry body. Before her eyes could even begin to adjust to the bright sunlight someone grasped her by the wrist and she yelped in fright.

'What kept you, slowcoach?' asked Joe as he let go of her arm. 'I thought you'd chickened out. We tried to come and fetch you, but we were having a bit of trouble finding the way back through.'

'What do you mean?' Jemima started to panic and took a step backwards, surprised to find herself half-in and half-out of the misty cloud. Heaving a sigh of relief she walked forward once more. 'Phew, it's okay,' she said. 'I thought we were going to be stuck in here.'

'See, I told you there was nothing to worry about,' replied Joe. 'Charlie and I probably weren't in the right place before, that's all.'

'Well, I just hope we manage to find the right place when we want to come back again,' she snapped, still worrying about what they were letting themselves in for. 'Don't forget to make a careful note of what's on the other side because we're probably going to need some sort of landmark we can recognise.'

'Yeah, yeah, stop going on about it and just try to enjoy yourself.'

# Chapter 3

Her earlier fears were completely swept aside as Jemima gazed about in awe, unable to believe her eyes. Joe was right – it was like stepping into the pages of a travel brochure. The three of them were standing on a sea shore with all sorts of hustle and bustle going on around them; fishing boats were pulled up on the sand and their crews hauled the daily catch ashore, while women scurried backwards and forwards carrying large woven baskets, helping to unload the fish. At the far end of the beach they spotted a group of children playing some sort of game with sticks and pebbles. Jemima thought it looked a bit like hopscotch, but with a dose of chase thrown in for good measure. Narrowing her eyes, she tried to pinpoint the exact spot where they'd just stepped out of the mist, fixing it in her memory for when they needed to go home again.

Entranced by the exotic smells and colours and feeling the hot sun warming her skin, Jemima stared up at the sky, which had to be the deepest shade of blue she'd ever seen. A sudden shout brought her back down to earth and she caught sight of Max being chased off one of the boats by an angry fisherman. The cat came bounding towards her proudly carrying a small fish in his mouth, which he'd managed to snaffle from the man's catch. He settled down on the sand and proceeded to devour his prize.

The children who'd been playing at the other end of the beach now moved closer, gesturing towards the three new arrivals and chattering all the while at breakneck speed. One girl of about their age, with shoulder-length dark hair and smiling brown eyes, approached them and pointing at Max, who was still polishing off his ill-gotten gains, she spoke to Jemima. However, the words sounded like complete gibberish - whatever language she was speaking, Jemima found it totally incomprehensible.

'I'm sor-ry, I don't un-der-stand,' enunciated Jemima, slowly and loudly in the way many grown-ups do if they're on holiday abroad in a country where they can't speak the language. The girl looked puzzled by what Jemima had said until Joe interrupted.

'Yes, he *is* a cat, just a rather large one, and he's called Max.' On hearing Joe's reply her face split into a wide grin and she answered him with yet another stream of words which meant nothing to Jemima or Charlie. 'Of course you can,' said Joe. 'He won't mind.' At this the girl knelt down and began to stroke Max, who rolled on to his back in the sand, purring ecstatically.

Jemima and Charlie stared at Joe in utter amazement.

'How on earth did you know what she said?' asked Charlie. 'It sounded like complete gobbledygook to me.'

'I couldn't understand a single word either,' added Jemima, mystified. As far as she knew her brother didn't speak any foreign languages.

Joe narrowed his eyes, regarding them as if they were stupid. 'What's wrong with you two? She speaks English, doesn't she?' Jemima and Charlie both shook their heads.

'Nope,' answered Charlie. 'She definitely wasn't speaking any form of English I recognised.'

'And she understood you too, Joe, but when I tried to speak to her she didn't know what I was saying,' said Jemima. She turned again towards the dark-haired girl who was still sitting on the sand making a fuss of Max.

'Hello, my name's Jemima. What's yours?'

The other girl looked up at her, a blank expression on her face.

'And I'm Charlie.' He accompanied this with a shy wave of his hand.

The girl frowned at him before turning to Joe, waiting for him to translate. Joe explained what Jemima and Charlie had said and she laughed with delight, pointing at herself and saying, 'Varna.' Then she said it again more slowly before gesturing to Jemima, obviously asking her name. Jemima obliged, stating her Christian name as clearly as possible. 'Jem-i-ma,' repeated Varna. Jemima's name sounded funny the way Varna pronounced it and everyone laughed. They carried out the same process with Charlie and Joe, until all the introductions had been made. Varna stood up and ran over to the other group of children who had edged closer by now, chattering in an excited voice as she told them about the visitors.

Meanwhile Jemima and Charlie were still trying to work out why Joe could communicate with Varna but they couldn't.

Varna returned, accompanied by the rest of her friends who were all dressed in short tunics of various colours and simple leather sandals. She made the introductions and Joe had to translate while the local children bombarded them with all sorts of questions. *Where had they come from? Why were they wearing such odd clothes*? Of course, no one there had ever seen tee-shirts, jeans and trainers before. *And why did Charlie have jewellery on his face*? This last question puzzled Joe, Jemima and Charlie for a moment until they realised the children meant his glasses. Joe explained how the lenses helped Charlie see more clearly and Charlie handed his spectacles over so they could all inspect them. Everyone agreed, however, after trying the glasses on, that everything looked much more blurry through the special lenses and couldn't understand why Charlie chose to wear such strange things.

Joe left out the bit about the old book and the misty cloud they'd stepped into, but explained they were visitors from another country. He thought if he told their new friends they were also visitors from another time – the future – it might freak them out. Unsurprisingly none of the children had ever heard of England and wondered aloud whether it was further away than Egypt.

'Oh yes,' said Joe. 'Much further than Egypt.' He turned to Varna. 'And what's this place called?'

'Atlantis, of course. Even you travellers from so far away must have heard of Atlantis?' replied a bemused Varna, looking at them sideways.

'Ah, yes. I thought so, but I just wanted to check we'd arrived in the right place,' he said quickly, casting a triumphant glance in Jemima and Charlie's direction.

At that moment a man standing near one of the fishing boats called out, waving his arm at the children. Varna beckoned to a boy of about seven or eight years old.

'This is my brother Mykos,' she explained, as he came to stand next to Joe, a wide grin revealing his two missing front teeth. 'We've got to go now and help our father tidy up his nets, but after we've finished you can come back to our house with us. I'm sure our parents would love to meet you. Will you stay here for a while and I'll fetch you when we're ready?'

'Okay,' replied Joe. 'See you later.' Varna and Mykos ran off in the direction of the boats, as the rest of the local children trotted away with friendly waves.

'Tell us, tell us,' said Jemima impatiently. 'What did she say?' She was still rather cross that only Joe seemed to be able to understand and they had to wait for him to translate everything for them.

'We are definitely in Atlantis,' replied Joe, with a wide grin.

'Awesome,' exclaimed Charlie. 'So it was a real place after all. Wait till we get back and tell everyone where we've been.'

'Nobody will believe us,' said Jemima. 'Not without proof anyway. People think Atlantis only existed in a myth and, if we say we've actually been there, they'll just laugh and say we're making it up.'

'I still don't understand how we got here,' said Charlie.

'Have we really travelled back in time?'

'I think it's all to do with the old book,' declared Joe. 'The whole thing, from the key to stepping into that weird cloud, is like something out of a science fiction story. I don't understand either, but what's worrying me most is how Atlantis disappeared. The entire place vanished off the face of the earth, which is why nobody knows its location or whether it actually existed at all. Something terrible happened here, didn't it? It destroyed the city and killed all the inhabitants.'

'Crikey,' exclaimed Charlie. 'Whatever it was, I hope it doesn't happen before we leave.'

'What about the people who live here and those children we've just met?' said Jemima. 'We ought to try and warn them if we can.'

'Well, later on we've been invited to Varna's house,' answered Joe. 'Let's try and work out how we can explain. I can't imagine they'll believe us though,' he added thoughtfully, looking down at his feet and prodding a pebble across the sand with the toe of his trainer.

The three children lay down on the beach, discussing the situation and trying to come up with some ideas. Jemima shuffled closer to Max who was still sleeping off his meal. The cat's warm, furry body made a comfortable pillow and before long her eyelids started to droop.

# Chapter 4

They must have all dozed off. Awoken by the sound of Varna's voice the three of them sat up rubbing their eyes, wondering where they were for a moment before remembering what had happened.

'Are you ready?' she asked. 'My father says you're more than welcome to come to our house and he's looking forward to meeting you – he loves hearing travellers' tales. We have a tradition here that all visitors must be treated with respect and that's why in our language we use the same word for both "stranger" and "guest". Come on, let's go.'

Joe translated what Varna had said, then he, Jemima and Charlie stood up, brushing the sand off their clothes. Jemima also did her best to get it all out of Max's fur, making him look as smart as possible. Following Varna and Mykos off the beach they headed into a small, winding street which led uphill towards the town, staring around in wonder as they walked.

'It's like something from a history book, or one of those

views of Bethlehem you get on Christmas cards,' whispered Jemima.

'No cars or bikes, just donkeys,' commented Joe.

'I wish I'd got sunglasses on,' said Charlie. 'These white houses are a bit dazzling, aren't they?'

Making their way into the town they soon realised everything seemed to be painted white, probably to reflect the sun and keep the buildings cool. After a few twists and turns Varna came to a halt before an open doorway in a narrow alleyway. Mykos caught sight of a friend sitting outside his house further up the alley and went to speak to him.

'This is our home,' said Varna proudly. On the wall next to the doorframe was a terracotta plaque bearing the design of a fish with three strange symbols underneath.

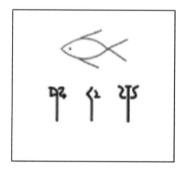

'Are these letters?' asked Joe as he traced his fingers over their outline.

'Of course. What did you think they were?'

'Your alphabet is completely different from ours,' he remarked.

'That's our house sign to show Medon the fisherman lives here,' explained Varna. 'Please come in.'

They stepped through the doorway and were instantly struck by the coolness of the interior. As their eyes adjusted to the darkness after the bright sunlight outside, a man standing in the centre of the single room appeared out of the shadows, smiling broadly and extending outstretched hands towards them in welcome. The smile died on his face, however, as he caught sight of Max cowering behind them.

'*Oh no,*' thought Jemima, as she recognised the fisherman from the beach, whose catch Max had helped himself to. Fortunately, a slow grin started to spread across the man's face and he began to laugh, wagging his finger at Max who peeped nervously round Jemima's legs, wondering if he should make a run for it.

'I suppose you'd like another one of my fishes would you, Mr Furry Thief?'

Varna and Joe started to giggle and, although she hadn't understood the words, Jemima realised with a sense of relief that Varna's father didn't seem angry after all and she joined in the laughter.

A woman, holding a toddler on her hip, appeared behind him and stepped shyly forward, smiling at the visitors. Like her daughter, Varna, she had dark hair and friendly brown eyes. Varna's mother gestured to them to take a seat at a large wooden table and they arranged themselves on the simple benches set either side, whilst she fetched clay bowls of olives, dates and cooked fish. She also brought two flat loaves of bread, while Varna went back into the street calling for Mykos to come home.

At last everyone was seated, apart from Max who'd been given his own clay bowl on the floor, containing some of the cooked fish. Varna's father indicated they should help themselves, but Jemima hesitated.

'Where's the cutlery?' she whispered.

'I think you're meant to use your fingers,' answered Charlie in a low voice.

'Cool,' said Joe. 'I always used to get told off for that at home.' He began to dig in enthusiastically.

Jemima wasn't too sure about the olives. They tasted a little bitter and she also found them fiddly to eat because of the stone inside. Nevertheless, she tucked into the rest of the food, suddenly realising how hungry she was. All this travel certainly gives you an appetite, she thought, glancing down at Max who'd just polished off his second helping of fish that day. He seemed to be making himself quite at home; licking his paws, he first smoothed back his whiskers and then proceeded to wash each ear in turn, before curling up on a rug for a little post-dinner snooze. Jemima had once read somewhere that cats can sleep for about twenty hours every day and she could well believe it if Max was anything to go by.

As they were eating, Joe thanked Varna's parents for their hospitality and then Varna's father began to speak.

'My name is Medon, my wife is called Aramina and our baby's name is Simi - obviously you've already met our two other children. We're all honoured to have you in our home. Whereabouts are you staying in Atlantis?' When Joe told him he wasn't sure yet, Medon immediately insisted they must all stay here with the family. Joe translated Medon's words for the benefit of the other two and at once Jemima started to worry.

'Shouldn't we be getting back? What'll happen when Mrs Garland finds out we're gone? Uncle Richard will be so mad at us for disappearing.'

'Shh,' said Joe 'I thought we'd agreed that we had to stay and help the people here. We've got to try and save them, remember. Besides, we can't leave now - it would be rude. We'll explain everything when we get back. I'm sure Uncle

Richard will understand. After all he knows all about ancient history, different customs and things, doesn't he? Anyway, I don't want to go home yet – this is far too much fun.'

With that he turned away from her and accepted Medon's kind invitation saying, 'Thank you. We'd love to stay.' Jemima, however, couldn't shake off her growing sense of unease. Despite the heat, a feeling of intense cold gripped her for an instant.

'Varna will take you on a tour of the city tomorrow, if you'd like,' said Medon. 'But for now she'll show you where you can sleep tonight.' He seemed a little surprised that the children had brought nothing with them at all in the way of belongings.

'Um, we left our things on the boat we arrived on,' said Joe, seeing the puzzled expression on Medon's face and thinking he ought to make something up to explain how they'd turned up here with only the clothes they stood up in. 'I'll go back down to the harbour tomorrow to collect them.'

Varna led the way up a narrow staircase and they emerged into a large upstairs room.

'Usually the whole family sleeps in this bedroom,' explained Varna. Unlike downstairs where there'd been no windows at all, at least up here some light filtered in through a small window, although Jemima noticed it didn't appear to have any glass. In one corner of the room a wooden stepladder led up to a trapdoor in the ceiling and Varna started to climb the steps, gesturing to them to follow. 'But when the weather's hot we often sleep up here on the roof.'

They clambered up behind her and found themselves on a flat terrace where canopies made of rough material, suspended on wooden posts, acted as a form of shelter above their heads. Leaning over the low parapet the children surveyed the view. Looking towards the sea they could see a harbour filled with boats bobbing about on the blue water and, in the opposite direction, further up the hill stood a large building flanked by square towers, its walls of white marble glittering in the rays of the setting sun.

'That's the royal palace,' said Varna, following their gaze. 'I'll take you up there tomorrow.'

Jemima hopped from one leg to the other several times before giving Joe a sharp nudge. 'Um, I need the loo. Will you find out where it is?' She blushed a little, feeling rather embarrassed at having to ask.

Joe put the question to Varna who first of all pointed to a large clay pot on one side of the roof terrace, but seeing the stricken expression on Jemima's face, beckoned to her to follow her back downstairs. She led her outside and through a little side alley next to the house. A gate opened into a yard

43

in the corner of which stood a small hut. Varna pointed to the door of the hut and Jemima peered inside. At first she recoiled in horror. Primitive didn't even begin to describe it and the smell made her wrinkle her nose in disgust, but at least there seemed to be some sort of wooden seat with a hole cut in it. She couldn't wait any longer, so she ventured inside while Varna waited for her by the gate.

Jemima sincerely hoped she wouldn't wake up in the night and need to go to the loo. No way could she come all the way down here in the dark. Feeling hugely relieved for now, however, she followed Varna back to rejoin the others. On the way, she collected Max, who'd also had to go outside to find somewhere to relieve himself. Being rather a fastidious cat he hoped they'd soon be going home to civilisation, where he had his own litter tray fitted with a lid and a door. He was definitely of the opinion that cats need their privacy where certain matters are concerned.

Once more up on the roof, with the glowing sky rapidly giving way to a velvety darkness, Varna made sure they all had a straw-stuffed mattress and a blanket each, before wishing them good night.

'Well, you can't say we're not having an adventure,' said Joe.

'I just hope my Mum isn't too worried,' said Charlie.

44

'What if she calls the police?' He gulped at the thought.

They took off their jeans, deciding it would be too hot to wear them during the night and lay down on the rough mattresses.

*I'll never be able to get to sleep up here*, thought Jemima as she cuddled up to Max's comforting warmth. In an instant, however, she'd drifted off, as had the boys. They were all exhausted by their adventures that day. Max, needless to say, was already fast asleep, snoring quietly in the way cats sometimes do.

# Chapter 5

Jemima was awoken the next morning by a wet nose pressed against her cheek, followed by a soft leather paw gently touching her eyelid. For a minute or two she had completely forgotten where she was, then as she took in her surroundings she remembered the events of the previous day.

'Hello, Max.' She stroked the familiar furry face as a pair of luminous aquamarine eyes gazed into her own. Pushing herself up on to one elbow she turned towards the slumbering form of her brother. 'Joe, wake up!' she hissed.

He grunted and opened one eyelid, squinting back at her, but as he became aware of where they were his eyes opened wider. 'So it wasn't a dream,' he whispered.

Charlie also began to stir and they all decided to get up, as noises coming from downstairs told them the family was already up and about.

'I've got to go and find the loo,' said Joe, scrambling into his jeans and hurrying down the stepladder.

What he didn't realise was that, when he grabbed his trousers to put them on, the little leather pouch containing the four golden charms had fallen out of his pocket and now lay on the floor. Charlie spotted the small leather bag straightaway and picked it up, calling to Joe as he did so. Joe's needs, however, were more urgent and he didn't hear, so Charlie put the pouch into his own pocket. 'I'll give it back to him downstairs.,' he said.

When Joe arrived on the ground floor he found Aramina and Varna seated at the table. Medon had already left several hours earlier to put out to sea in his fishing boat.

'How did you sleep?' asked Varna.

Well, that's what she said, but Joe didn't actually understand a single word. He shook his head, thinking he must still be half-asleep and, pointing through the open doorway, he dashed outside to find the toilet.

Meanwhile Jemima and Charlie made their way downstairs to be greeted by the smiling faces of Varna and her family.

'Would you like some breakfast?' asked Varna in a slow, clear voice, but nevertheless in her native Atlantean language. Without thinking Charlie automatically replied, 'Yes please.' As Varna stared back at him in astonishment Charlie realised, equally amazed, that he knew what she'd

47

said to him and she, in turn, had understood his reply. Varna shook herself and gestured to them to sit down. Jemima looked from one to the other in disbelief.

'You understood her,' she whispered in an accusing tone. 'How come? Yesterday you told me you didn't understand a thing.' Jemima felt extremely miffed. Was she going to end up being the odd one out now, understanding nothing while the two boys got on like a house on fire with all the local people?

'I don't know what's happened,' shrugged Charlie. 'I can understand her perfectly today.' Jemima scowled at him.

Varna smiled, but looked puzzled as she brought them plates of bread, together with a bowl of honey - not the sort from a jar, but real fresh honeycomb that Jemima had only ever seen in pictures. A large jug also stood on the table and Varna picked it up, pouring milk into earthenware beakers for them. Jemima was thirsty, but as she took a long drink she pulled a bit of a face, wrinkling her nose.

'Oh, it tastes strange!' she exclaimed. 'It's not like normal milk.'

Varna seemed worried by the expression on Jemima's face, so Charlie told her what Jemima had said.

'But this is normal milk,' explained Varna, sniffing the jug to make sure it hadn't gone off. 'It's not strange.'

In fact, it turned out to be goats' milk which they found delicious once they got used to the taste – sweet and creamy – and Jemima held out her beaker for a re-fill which seemed to please Varna. They were both tucking into their breakfast when Joe reappeared.

'Come and eat, Joe,' said Varna.

Joe, however, stood blinking in the doorway. Something odd was going on. Varna seemed to be speaking to him, but he couldn't understand a single word.

'Er ... I'll come and sit down shall I?'

Varna, in turn, hadn't a clue what he'd just said and was baffled. Joe had spoken fluent Atlantean yesterday. What was he playing at?

He joined the others at the table. 'I don't understand,' he whispered. 'Something weird is going on here.' As he sat down, he gave a sudden gasp and put his hand into the pocket of his jeans. 'Oh no, the pouch is gone. I must have dropped it outside.' He started to get up.

'Don't worry, Joe, I found it upstairs. Here you are,' said Charlie, handing over the small purse.

'Phew! Thanks, Charlie. I'll be more careful with it from now on.'

'Well, when we've all had breakfast I can show you around Atlantis, if you'd like,' said Varna, returning to the

49

table. She addressed this to Charlie as he'd seemed to understand earlier. But now he gave no sign of understanding her at all and just gaped at her like a goldfish, his mouth opening and closing, but no sound coming out. The silence which followed was broken by Joe. Without even looking up and with his mouth stuffed full of bread and honey as he concentrated on the important matter of breakfast, he answered Varna's question.

'Yes, that would be great. Thanks.' He became aware of everyone staring at him rather oddly and he raised his head, looking from one to the other. Realising what had happened, he found himself as taken aback as they were. This was just too strange for words.

'First you understand Atlantean, then you don't and now you do again,' said Jemima crossly. 'And Charlie does the complete opposite. Are you two messing about, because, if you are, it's not funny?' She glared at them both with a grumpy expression on her face.

'Joe, give me back that pouch again for a moment would you?' said Charlie.

'Why?'

'Just a small experiment,' replied Charlie, as Joe fished in his pocket and gave him the leather purse. 'Say something, Varna.'

'What would you like me to say?' she asked, puzzled.

'Nothing. That's enough.' He smiled mysteriously at the others. 'Shall we help you clear the table?' As he said this he passed the pouch to Jemima.

'No, thank you,' answered Varna. 'You go and get ready to go out while I give my mother a hand for a few minutes.' She turned away, thinking these foreigners seemed a little peculiar at times. Perhaps everyone was like that in their country. She didn't spot Jemima staring at her open-mouthed.

'I can understand,' gasped Jemima, 'Why? What...?'

'I'll tell you upstairs,' replied Charlie, tapping the side of his nose with his forefinger and winking at her.

They scuttled back up to the roof terrace, eager to hear Charlie's explanation. Max arose from the rug he was lounging on and followed them. He'd been just about to settle down for a little snooze after his breakfast, but he didn't want the children to leave him behind – he might miss something interesting.

# Chapter 6

'So,' began Joe, once they'd arrived back on the roof, 'You're saying this is all to do with the leather pouch. Whoever's holding it can understand the local language and the local people can understand them too, which explains everything. We'll just have to take it in turns.'

'I think I've got a better idea,' said Jemima. 'What if the important thing isn't the pouch itself, but the owl charms inside it? We could all keep one and, hey presto, the problem's solved.'

Joe untied the drawstring, tipping the contents on to a blanket and they each took one of the four golden birds.

'We must be careful not to lose them,' said Charlie.

Jemima undid the clasp on her necklace. 'No problem,' she declared. 'I'll put mine on here with the key.' She threaded the chain through the loop on the top of the bird's head, before putting it back round her neck. 'You two can think of something else to do with yours. Hang on, how about this for an idea? If you take the shoelace off one of your trainers, you might be able to make a cord by pulling apart the threads. Then you can put it through the loop in the charm and tie the cord round your neck.'

'I'm not wearing girly jewellery,' protested Joe. 'And besides my trainer will fall off.'

'You can hide the necklace under your tee shirt and, if you cut the other shoelace in half, there'll be enough left over to lace up both trainers.'

The boys each unlaced one of their shoes and did as Jemima suggested.

'Now go downstairs and find a knife that you can use to cut your other shoelaces with,' she said. 'There's one charm to spare though. What shall we do with it?' A soft yowl from the direction of one of the beds attracted their attention and they looked across at Max who was regarding them hopefully, sitting as upright as possible and stretching his chin upwards. Jemima glanced at the cat and then back at the charm in her hand. She instinctively knew what he wanted her to do and went over to him. 'Okay, Max, but you mustn't lose this whatever you do,' she said as she attached the golden owl to his collar.

At once, in a soft voice, they heard him say, 'Well, that took you long enough to work out.'

The children all gasped, staring at the large cat in

disbelief.

'Max, you can talk,' said Jemima, awestruck.

'I've always been able to talk, Jemima, but you just didn't understand me,' he answered with a small sniff.

Jemima immediately enfolded him in a rib-crushing hug, planting a big kiss on the top of his head as she did so. 'I *love* you, Max.'

'I know, I know. You've told me often enough,' he replied in a slightly gruff voice. 'I love you too,' he added in a whisper.

Jemima's eyes glistened with tears. She'd always suspected he was trying to speak to her and he clearly understood everything they said to him. She'd been right all along.

Charlie stared at Max in admiration. 'Awesome! A talking cat – you guys are so lucky.' Max rolled his eyes.

'Come on,' said Joe. 'Let's go back downstairs and deal with our shoelaces. Oh, and Max, best not to speak in front of anybody else. I'm not sure how they might react to a cat who can talk.'

# Chapter 7

Varna's mother gave them an apple each and the four children went out of the house. Instead of heading back down towards the sea, they turned left and started climbing up in the direction of the palace they'd seen from the roof terrace. Already the sun had risen high in the sky and Jemima soon began to complain about the heat.

'At least you're not wearing a fur coat,' muttered Max who was trotting along beside her.

Varna kept her surprise to herself that all three of the visitors now spoke perfect Atlantean and seemed to have no difficulty understanding what she said to them. Of course they were foreigners, but maybe there was more to it than them just being from another country. She considered the possibility the three strangers might have been sent by the gods or they could even be gods themselves. Everyone knew how the immortal family liked to disguise themselves as mortals sometimes – just for fun – but then why should they bother with someone as ordinary as her? Varna chided herself for letting her imagination run wild and decided to concentrate on enjoying her day out with her new friends.

Unsurprisingly, the local inhabitants stared with undisguised curiosity at the three visitors, who looked nothing like anyone they'd ever seen before. The Atlanteans were used to foreign merchants, such as Egyptians and Phoenicians, who came in their ships to trade, but these children were beyond different and people whispered behind their hands as they passed – those strange clothes, the funny pale hair and the odd-looking things that boy was wearing over his eyes. Odder still was the large creature lolloping along at the girl's side: it had the pointed features of a cat but was the size of a dog. No, it was generally agreed, no one had ever seen quite such a strange bunch, but recognising Varna, they all gave friendly waves as the children passed.

Varna led the way, acting as their guide. 'That's the bakery we get our bread from,' she said, gesturing at an open shop front. 'And here's the house where Mykos' friend Patros lives.'

Winding their way up the narrow streets towards the royal palace, they came to a square dominated by a grand building, rather like a smaller version of the Parthenon, the famous temple in Athens. Built of shining white marble, soaring columns supported a pediment decorated with carved figures of men and bulls and in the centre sat the large image of a bearded man holding a trident, flanked by winged horses. All the carving was picked out in bold colours, making the whole scene stand out vividly against the white stone. On a rectangular plaque beneath the carving were five strange symbols. Jemima had to shield her eyes against the brightness of the sun reflecting off the white stone. She gazed at the building in awe.

'I wish we'd brought a camera with us,' she said. 'Just imagine if we could have taken a picture of this place. People would have had to believe us then, wouldn't they?'

Joe and Charlie nodded, equally impressed by the beautiful structure.

'This is the Temple of Poseidon,' explained Varna. 'You can see his name written up there.' She pointed to the carving on the pediment.

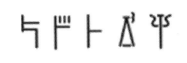

Joe stared at the strangely-shaped symbols, thinking how weird their alphabet seemed.

'I've heard of Poseidon,' said Charlie. 'He was the god of

the sea, wasn't he?'

'He still *is* the god of the sea,' said Varna, correcting him. 'Surely you worship the gods where you come from, don't you?' She regarded the boys sideways, a suspicious expression on her face.

'Ah, I think we call them by different names in our country,' replied Joe quickly.

'Oh, of course,' she answered. 'We have a goddess named Neith, whom the Athenians call Athena, but she's exactly the same.'

As they stood admiring the temple, Varna explained that the sea-god Poseidon, the brother of Zeus, was the protector of Atlantis. 'According to Atlantean legend our royal family is descended from Poseidon himself,' she said proudly. 'His eldest son, Atlas, became our first king and Atlantis was named after him.'

'Can we have a look inside?' asked Joe. Varna turned to him with a shocked expression.

'Inside? Are you mad? It's absolutely forbidden. The temple is sacred – only the priests are permitted to enter the god's private sanctuary. Don't tell me you're allowed inside the temples in your country?'

Joe coughed. 'Um, only a few of them,' he answered. 'I just wondered if the rules were different in Atlantis.'

'I think we'd better move on,' announced Varna, shaking her head. *For heaven's sake, some of the things these foreigners came out with! What a good job no priests were out here listening to their conversation* – or so she thought. None of them had spotted the robed figure lurking just inside the temple, who'd overheard every word and who now stood rubbing his chin thoughtfully.

The children carried on walking and Varna continued to point out places of local interest as they climbed upwards.

'The Law Court is on the left,' she said. 'And opposite is the prison cell where condemned prisoners are kept until their execution.'

They all stared at the small, square building with its solid-looking wooden door. It didn't seem to have any windows, so must be horribly dark inside, thought Jemima, shuddering as she considered the poor people who were locked in there awaiting their fate.

'Are there any prisoners in there right now and how are they put to death?' asked Joe, with ghoulish interest.

Jemima rolled her eyes. Why are boys always so keen to know the gruesome details?

'No, it's been empty for quite a long time now because life is peaceful in Atlantis these days,' said Varna. 'Though my grandfather used to tell us stories about the war against the Athenians, when they used to put captured prisoners to death. The executioners killed the captives with swords or strangled them in the main square. Sometimes, if they were high-ranking Athenian nobles, they were offered poison to swallow by themselves.'

'Ugh!' said Charlie. 'Strangled, stabbed or forced to commit suicide, I'm not sure which is worse. I'm glad that all happened a long time ago.'

'I don't think the people of Atlantis have quite got over their mistrust of the Athenians completely though,' said Varna. 'They're always on the lookout for spies because everyone's so frightened of such a horrible war breaking out again.'

They continued their progress up the hill until, rounding a final bend in the street, they found themselves in front of the royal palace. From a distance the building had been spectacular enough, but up close it appeared a hundred times more breathtaking. The walls rose up so high it was impossible see the top of them, and each side of the grand entrance was flanked by soaring towers. Again, the vast expanse of glittering white marble was almost too bright to look at. All the stones surrounding the immense doorway were adorned with gold and the rich blue of lapis lazuli, leaving the children to imagine how beautiful the interior must be. This time, however, even Joe had the good sense not to ask if they could go inside.

'From up here there's a fantastic view down over the city,' said Varna with a sweep of her hand. 'The palace is built on the "acropolis", which is what we call the highest part of the town. We're surrounded by the sea, but you can also see our fields and vineyards. We're lucky that crops grow easily here and anything we can't produce ourselves we buy from the traders' ships.'

Jemima, Joe and Charlie followed Varna's hand, admiring the stunning view.

'This would be one of the best holiday destinations in the world,' said Charlie, '...if it still existed,' he added quietly so that Varna didn't overhear.

'It's all so beautiful,' whispered Jemima wistfully. 'How awful to think the whole place is going to be destroyed. I wonder what happened exactly.' She shivered, despite the heat of the sun which now sat almost directly overhead.

Fortunately Varna didn't hear this comment either and turned towards them. 'I think we've seen enough for now. The weather's even hotter than usual today and you must be feeling tired and thirsty. Your faces have turned rather pink! Let's go home for something to eat and afterwards you can rest for a while. Later on we'll all go to the beach for a swim if you'd like.'

*Oh good*, thought Max, *food and sleep – my two favourite things. All this sightseeing is a bit hard on the paws too.*

They set off back down the hill, crossing the square in front of the Temple of Poseidon, but didn't notice the figure lurking in the shadows behind the columns at its entrance. He had noticed them, however, and narrowed his eyes as they passed. Hmm. These foreigners looked very strange indeed and as for the cat trailing behind ... certainly not an ordinary one by any stretch of the imagination. The sheer size of the creature and that long, pointed face made it seem more like a wild animal from the place the merchants called Africa.

All of a sudden Max felt his fur stand on end and he turned to look back towards the temple as they passed it. The figure withdrew deeper into the shadows inside. Max thought he must have been imagining things, in spite of the cold shiver which ran down his spine, and he ran to catch up with the children who'd carried on ahead.

Back at the house Varna filled a jug from the well in the yard. Everyone was thirsty, including Max who drank a whole bowl of the deliciously cool water in one go. After a tasty lunch of bread, soft white cheese and fruit, Varna suggested they go up to the roof terrace for a couple of hours' sleep. 'And then we can go down to the beach later,' she added.

Joe, Jemima and Charlie all thought this sounded like a good idea and they disappeared upstairs, accompanied by Max who was relishing the prospect of a lengthy post-lunch snooze.

# Chapter 8

The children sprawled on their mattresses, protected from the sun's glare by the canopy above them. However, the heat of the afternoon enveloped their bodies like a warm, heavy blanket making them all still feel rather dozy, in spite of having slept for at least two hours.

'What are we going to do?' asked Jemima. 'We can't stay here much longer and we haven't tried to warn Varna and her family about the disaster yet. And we've *really* got to go home soon; Uncle Richard must be frantic ... and Charlie's mum too.'

'Oh, we don't need to rush into anything,' answered Joe lazily, in no hurry to move from the comfy position he was lying in.

'Jemima's right, though,' said Charlie. 'We must think up some sort of plan. Let's try explaining everything to Medon this evening.'

'In my humble opinion...' began Max. They all jumped. Getting used to him talking would no doubt take quite a while. 'As I was about to say,' he continued, 'perhaps we should start with Varna this afternoon. Children are less set in their ways than grown-ups, as you know, and therefore more likely to believe unusual stories.'

'Good idea, Max,' said Joe. 'We'll tell her when we go to the beach.'

'There's one other thing I want to do before we leave here,' said Jemima. 'And that's to go back to the Temple of Poseidon. I know we haven't got a camera, but if I got some paper I'd like to make a sketch which we could use as evidence when we go home.'

'I don't think paper's been invented yet, Jemima,' scoffed Joe.

'But they might have papyrus like the Egyptians,' said Charlie. 'After all, the Atlanteans do trade with them. Maybe that's one of the things they import.'

'I don't suppose they've invented pencils yet either?' ventured Jemima.

'I'm sure we can find something to write with,' answered Charlie.

Max shivered as he heard Jemima say the word "temple". He still hadn't quite shaken off the sense of unease he'd experienced outside that place – an unpleasant feeling that someone or something inside had been watching them. He decided not to mention anything to the children, however. Best not to worry them unnecessarily.

Their discussion was interrupted by the sound of Varna's voice calling from below. 'Are you all awake? Who's for a swim?'

All thoughts of sleep banished, they scampered down the ladder to meet her.

******

The beach almost felt like familiar territory for the children. It would be so easy to step back into our own time from here, thought Jemima. Part of her longed to do exactly that, although she was enjoying being in Atlantis and, as Joe had said, it was proving to be a real adventure. With a jolt of guilt, she was amazed to realise she'd been too busy to think about her parents since she'd arrived and hadn't felt sad at all ... not once.

The children they'd met the day before, who included Varna's and Mykos' cousins as well as some of their friends who lived in the same street, were already on the beach when they arrived. Joe found a large dried-up sea sponge lying on the sand and he started kicking it about.

'Do you know how to play football, Mykos?' he asked.

Mykos shook his head, mystified. Joe began kicking the sponge around and the others gradually began to join in. Soon they'd marked out goalposts using pairs of sandals and, once Joe had explained the rules, everyone quickly got the hang of it. Even Charlie, who wasn't particularly sporty, found himself being roped in and enjoying himself.

'You should call this game footsponge, not football,' laughed Mykos with delight as he kicked the sponge enthusiastically, scoring an impressive goal.

An hour went by before the tired and overheated children finally stopped playing. Some of them had to leave and the rest decided to go for a swim to cool off. Jemima had wandered along the beach, picking up shells and thinking about home. Joe and Charlie's whoops as they ran into the sea brought her back to reality, or at least the reality of where she was at the moment. The boys had stripped off and had plunged into the sea wearing just their underpants. No way was Jemima going to undress in public, but she took off her trainers and rolled up her jeans so that she could paddle. Varna meanwhile was swimming in her tunic.

'Do the same as me,' called Varna. 'Your clothes will dry quickly in the sun afterwards.'

Jemima shook her head, preferring to splash about in the shallows. Max, however, wasn't too keen on getting wet and chose to watch the children at a safe distance from the water's edge. After a while, Jemima made her way back up the beach and plonked herself down next to him with a faraway expression on her face.

'Keep those wet feet well away from me,' grumbled Max. As she settled down by his side with a small sigh, he turned towards her noting the wistful look in her eyes. 'There's something I need to tell you, Jemima,' he began in a gentler voice. 'Your parents aren't dead you know. They're just lost.'

She gasped and turned to stare at him. 'What on earth do you mean?'

'Your mum and dad went travelling too, but weren't able to get home again. They're not far away, Jemima. Keep on looking and one day you'll find them.'

Tears welled up in Jemima's eyes. 'Is that true, Max? They're still alive? Really?'

'Yes, really,' he replied quietly.

Then it dawned on her just what Max was trying to say. 'Has it got something to do with the book? Did Mum and Dad do the same as us? Are they here in Atlantis?'

'Yes, yes and ... no – in that order,' said Max. 'Your parents did come to Atlantis, but I think they've moved on to somewhere else now. You and Joe will have to rescue them.'

'Rescue them?' gasped Jemima. 'Why? Are they in danger?'

'No,' said Max. 'Not as such, but they can't return, not without the key which they left behind by mistake. I was there and saw everything. I just haven't been able to tell anyone about it ... until now.'

Jemima looked puzzled for an instant and then, as realisation dawned, she reached inside her tee shirt and closed her hand around her necklace.

'Is this the key? Did I really hear my mum's voice telling me to pick it up? Has she been trying to talk to me?'

'I think so,' said Max softly.

Tears rolled down Jemima's cheeks, but she felt happier than she had for months. She flung herself at Max and hugged him tightly.

'Thank you, thank you. I can't wait to tell Joe.'

Max's fur soaked up her tears and he let her sob for a little while before giving her face a gentle bump with his head.

'Come on, Jemima. Pull yourself together now. We've got a job to do here in Atlantis and you must be strong.'

'Okay.' She snuffled a little, but sat up, her eyes shining and a broad smile lighting up her features.

Joe, Charlie and Varna emerged dripping from the sea

and ran over to join Jemima. Seeing her tear-stained but beaming face Joe looked at her questioningly.

'I'll tell you later,' she murmured.

The boys shook themselves like dogs, rather alarming Max, and sat down on the sand. 'We need to talk to you about something, Varna,' said Joe. 'Come and sit next to us.'

# Chapter 9

Varna stared from one to the other with a worried expression on her face.

'This is rather difficult to explain,' began Joe. 'But we've got to warn you about something that's going to happen to Atlantis. I'm afraid you're all in terrible danger.'

'Is it the Athenians?' she asked. 'Are they planning to invade us again? What's it got to do with you? Are you spies? Do you ...?'

'Listen, Varna,' interrupted Joe. 'It's nothing to do with the Athenians, okay? And, no, we're not spies.'

'I'm afraid it's far worse than that,' said Jemima. 'A matter of life and death in fact, but we're here to help.'

'Atlantis is going to be destroyed and it may happen quite soon,' added Charlie. 'You're going to find this hard to believe, but you'll have to trust us if you want to save your family and friends.'

'I don't understand,' said Varna. 'What could possibly happen to Atlantis? And anyway, how do you three know anything about this? You're not even from round here. You're talking nonsense and you're starting to frighten me. Who are you and why are you here?'

Clearly annoyed she started to scramble to her feet, but Jemima grabbed hold of her hand and pulled her gently back down. 'This is serious, Varna. Please don't be angry with us. We've been sent here to warn you, so everyone can escape. All we know is that Atlantis is going to be flooded and will disappear for ever.'

At first Varna just scoffed in disbelief. How could somewhere as solid as Atlantis disappear? But as she studied them more closely she saw genuine concern written on their faces and then she remembered her earlier thoughts about their strange behaviour.

'Who sent you here with this information and why?' she asked.

'Ah, we can't actually tell you that,' replied Joe, wondering what he might say to convince her.

'As I thought,' she said. 'I'll bet you're messengers from the gods.'

Joe, Jemima and Charlie glanced at each other, not knowing how to answer this. Varna, however, took their silence as confirmation. 'I understand,' she continued. 'You're not allowed to tell me, but this explains everything about you all turning up here out of the blue and behaving so oddly. We must go home and talk to my mother and father. They'll know what to do.'

*******

As expected, Varna's parents weren't in a hurry to believe "children's fairy tales", as Medon called them. He stood up impatiently, saying he had more important things to be getting on with. Aramina, however, reached for his hand to stop him.

'Wait a moment, Medon. It isn't the first time there's been a warning like this. Remember the two people who came here about six months ago? They weren't children, were they?'

'No,' he replied curtly. 'And, if you recall, the priests chased them out of town for being troublemakers. Those people couldn't even speak our language and they expected us to take note of their silly drawings and diagrams. Atlantis is a big place. Are we honestly supposed to believe the whole city will be swallowed up, together with all of its people? Pah!' He shook off his wife's hand and left the house, unsmiling for once.

Jemima sat frozen like a statue. A massive shock had run

73

through her body when Aramina had spoken about the two previous visitors to Atlantis.

'Are you all right, Jemima?' asked Joe, realising she'd been a little strange all afternoon.

'Um ... I'm fine, but I'd like to talk to you about something. Why don't we all go upstairs? I just need to have a quiet word with Aramina first, if that's okay?' She glanced across at Aramina who nodded back at her.

The others clattered off up the stairs, while Jemima remained seated opposite Varna's mother.

'We really are here to help,' she began. 'And we'll just have to find a way to prove we're telling the truth.'

'Thank you,' replied Aramina. 'We can never truly understand the ways of the gods and, if something dreadful *is* going to happen, then I want my family to escape.'

'Aramina?' said Jemima hesitantly. 'You mentioned two other foreigners a minute ago. Can you describe them for me?'

'Well, I remember a man and a woman who wore strange garments rather like yours and the lady had the same pale hair as you,' she said, reaching out a hand to stroke Jemima's ponytail. 'Perhaps they were from your country too? The man kept on trying to show us pictures of Atlantis being covered by the sea, but neither of them spoke any Atlantean so nobody was able to understand what it was all about. People got angry when they wouldn't give up and thought they might be spies sent to stir up unrest. Eventually the two of them ended up being chased away by a crowd led by the priests from the temple and didn't come back again.'

Jemima's eyes glistened with unshed tears and Aramina patted her hand, wondering what she'd said to upset her.

'Go on, she murmured. 'Go and join the others. See if you can come up with some sort of plan and I'll try to talk Medon round.'

Jemima smiled gratefully and got up. She climbed the stairs, with Max giving her a comforting nudge as she did so.

On the roof terrace Jemima took Joe to one side and pulled him down to sit next to her on one of the mattresses. In a whisper she told him about what Max and Aramina had said about their missing parents. His eyes filled with tears and he glanced across at Max, who nodded in confirmation. Stifling a sob, Jemima hugged him and they held on to each other for a few moments, both crying quietly. After a couple of minutes Joe searched Jemima's face hopefully. 'Is it really true?' he asked in a shaky voice. She nodded, giving him a watery smile.

'Yeeees!' He gave a sudden whoop and jumped up from

75

the mattress, punching the air with his fist. Charlie and Varna stared at him in surprise, wondering what was going on, while Max sat watching them all, wearing a grin that the Cheshire Cat would have been proud of.

# Chapter 10

Later that evening, after a meal eaten in rather uncomfortable silence, Medon cleared his throat and began to speak. 'Um...if you'd all stay seated for a moment I'd like to talk to you,' he said. 'I'm sorry if I sounded a little rude earlier. Aramina has persuaded me to give you another chance to explain. Perhaps you should start from the beginning and tell us everything.'

Joe glanced at Jemima and Charlie who nodded their encouragement. 'Well,' he began. 'We'll tell you what we know, which honestly isn't much. We're not trying to cause any trouble. We want to help you and you've been so kind to us we'd hate to see something terrible happen to you.'

'Get on with it, Joe,' hissed Jemima.

The family sat staring at Joe intently, their faces reflecting increasing disbelief as he recounted the tale of Atlantis which they'd read in the old book at home.

'...and so Atlantis is going to vanish forever and in the future people won't even be sure it ever truly existed. Its name will live on as a mere legend,' he concluded.

'But how do you know that?' asked Medon, still unconvinced. 'Where did *you* get this information and why should we believe you?'

'We can't make you,' answered Jemima. 'But we hope you'll realise we wouldn't lie to you. You're our friends.'

'I still don't understand how you're able to foretell the fate of Atlantis,' said Medon. 'Can you really see into the future?'

'We could tell you other things about the future you might find even harder to believe,' said Charlie. 'For example, thousands of years from now you'll be able to move from one city to another in a car, a four-wheeled machine which travels along roads faster than a galloping horse or even fly through the air in an aeroplane, a machine with wings which carries hundreds of people across the sky.'

'Pah! Now you're definitely making it up,' snorted Medon.

'Medon, I think I believe these children,' said Aramina quietly. 'We should try to save our family if what they're saying is true. Don't you want to do the same?'

After a few moments he began to nod slowly.

'I think those people who came here before were trying to warn us too,' continued Aramina. As she spoke she glanced across at Jemima, a kindly look in her eyes. Jemima gave her a grateful smile in return.

'So what do we do?' asked Medon.

'Well, we're not sure how much time we've got ...' began Joe.

'I thought you knew all about the destruction of Atlantis,' scoffed Medon. 'Can you predict the future or not?'

'We're certain a catastrophe will take place,' said Charlie. 'We're just not absolutely sure *when* it's going to happen.'

'So what's the rush?' asked Medon. 'You're asking us to leave our home and our life here for something which might not happen for years.'

'I'm not willing to stay and take the risk, Medon,' said Aramina. 'I want our children to grow up to lead long and happy lives. Don't you? Please let's think about it.'

Grudgingly Medon nodded once more and took hold of his wife's hand. 'First of all where would we go and secondly who else could we persuade to leave with us? Starting from scratch somewhere totally new won't be easy.'

'No,' she replied. 'But it's better than the alternative if we stay.'

'I suppose you're right,' he admitted. 'I may have an idea. Many of the merchants I meet down at the harbour are from Kriti and apparently that's a good place to live. It's not too far away either - maybe only a day and night at sea. We could manage that in our boat.'

'I've never heard of Kriti,' said Joe.

'A-ha, so you don't know everything then do you, young man?' laughed Medon. 'Kriti is a large island south of here, on the way to Egypt.'

'Actually, I think I do know where that is,' said Charlie.

Joe and Jemima looked at him in surprise.

'I went on holiday to Crete once with my Mum and Dad,' he explained. 'When I bought some postcards the name of the island was written on them in Greek and the lady in the shop told me it was pronounced "Kriti".'

'What are postcards?' asked Medon, looking puzzled.

'Oh, nothing important,' replied Joe. 'Anyway, Medon, Kriti sounds like a perfect place for you all to escape to.'

'Will you be coming with us too?' asked Medon. 'Surely you won't want to stay here if Atlantis is going to disappear like you say?'

'We'd love to come with you. That would be great ...' began Joe, eager to prolong this adventure for as long as possible.

'... But unfortunately we can't,' interrupted Jemima. 'We must go home. We've been away for far too long as it is.' She glared at her brother, daring him to contradict her.

Charlie breathed a sigh of relief: he had to agree with Jemima. This trip had been amazing, but he was already worried about facing his mum when he returned home, without staying away even longer. Joe did tend to get carried away far too easily, completely forgetting about the consequences.

I understand, but it will be a shame to say goodbye to you so soon,' said Medon. 'Well, now all we've got to do is decide who we can persuade to come with us,' said Medon. 'Getting them to believe us won't be easy. Remember how everyone reacted to the last people who tried to warn them? And we'll need several days to make all the preparations.'

'I just hope we've got that long,' muttered Joe. 'Listen, we'll pop out for a quick walk before bedtime. You've all got a lot to talk about and you can tell us what you've decided when we come back.'

Joe, Jemima and Charlie got up from the table, leaving the family to discuss the situation on their own, and went out into the street. Max trotted along at their heels, determined not to be left behind.

'Well, at least Medon seems to be taking us seriously at last,' said Jemima. 'I'm so glad we've managed to convince him.'

'Don't forget he's going to have a hard job getting their

friends to listen to him,' replied Joe. 'I hope he doesn't give up and decide to stay put. Come on, let's go up the road towards the temple.'

An involuntary shiver ran down Max's spine at the word "temple" and he stuck close to Jemima's legs as they set off along the lane.

'Once he's managed to persuade as many people as possible to leave we'll be able to go home again,' sighed Jemima. 'I dread to think of the trouble we're going to be in when we get back. We'll probably be grounded for the rest of our lives.'

They carried on walking until they reached the square where the Temple of Poseidon stood. Joe strolled over to the front of the building and plonked himself down on the lowest step.

'Let's sit here for a while,' he said. 'Then we can go back to the house and find out how they're getting on with their plans.'

A shadow moved in the darkness behind him and Max was certain he heard a hiss, like a sharp intake of breath.

'I'm not sure you should do that, Joe,' he whispered.

'What did you say, Max? I didn't quite catch it.'

'I said maybe you shouldn't do that,' repeated Max, a little more loudly. 'This is a sacred place, remember? Sitting there might not be allowed.'

'Nonsense,' replied Joe as he leaned back against the stone, completely unaware of the figure lurking behind one of the columns at the top of the steps.

The priest had overheard the conversation between Joe and Max, which only served to confirm his worst suspicions about the visitors. He frowned thoughtfully. *So, the animal had the power of speech – this was serious magic indeed and they would have to capture the creature as soon as possible. They couldn't have something like that roaming the streets of Atlantis, causing untold havoc. Just what were these strangers up to? Certainly nothing good, based on all this talk of plans being made. The high priest must hear of this at once.* He turned to disappear into the recesses of the temple, but only Max seemed to notice the swish of his robes as he went.

'Let's go back to the house now, Joe,' he pleaded.

'Whatever's the matter, Max?' asked Jemima. 'Anyone would think you'd seen a ghost.'

Jemima was right; his fur was standing on end as though he'd had an electric shock.

'I don't like it here,' said Max. 'This place gives me the creeps. Please, let's go.'

Jemima shuddered. It didn't take much to scare her and Max was so insistent that even the boys started looking nervously over their shoulders, beginning to feel uncomfortable.

'Okay,' said Joe. 'I guess we should be getting back anyway.'

As they set off down the lane, Max turned and cast one last look back towards the temple. He was sure he caught sight of a flash of blue material and the glitter of a pair of eyes in the darkness. Whatever was inside that place had to be bad news, he thought, and he scurried to keep up with the children as they made their way down the hill.

# Chapter 11

The next morning Medon left the house early. He needed to speak to as many people as possible about leaving Atlantis and Aramina hoped he'd be successful. She too had friends and relatives she wanted to talk into going with them and so also went out straight after breakfast, carrying baby Simi on her hip.

*It's going to be a real scorcher today*, thought Jemima, and the prospect of putting on her jeans and trainers again in this heat was almost too much to bear. Luckily Varna came to her rescue and brought her a faded yellow tunic and an old pair of sandals she'd outgrown. The clothes were a perfect fit and, although not the sort of thing she'd be seen dead in back home, Jemima instantly felt cooler and more comfortable. She knotted the cord belt around her waist and straightened the tunic, grinning to herself. She could almost pass for an Atlantean now, if it wasn't for her blonde hair of course.

'Let's go down to the harbour first and then move on to

the market,' said Varna. 'We'll have to tell everyone we meet. You never know, some of them might believe us.'

'Okay,' replied Jemima. 'I'll go and fetch the boys.'

After a bit of nagging and cajoling Joe and Charlie finally declared themselves ready.

'Like the outfit, Jem,' said Joe with a snigger as he sneered at her new clothes.

'I'll be the one laughing when you get too hot in your jeans and trainers,' she replied. 'Are you coming too, Max?' No response. 'Max?' she repeated, blowing softly into his ear. Still nothing. She shook him gently, only to be rewarded with a crotchety grumble. For goodness sake, she thought, cats are supposed to be alert at the slightest sound whereas Max behaved more like a grumpy old man if anyone interrupted his slumbers. She'd never known an animal sleep so deeply.

In truth, Max had suffered a rather sleepless night disturbed by nightmares involving that wretched temple and whatever was lurking inside, so was quite happy for them to go out, leaving him to enjoy a much-needed lie-in.

Jemima put some breakfast in a bowl for him and then they all headed down towards the harbour. The waterside was heaving with activity and Joe, Jemima and Charlie soon found themselves overwhelmed by the exotic sights, sounds and smells which assailed their senses. Everywhere they looked men were busy loading and unloading boats with all manner of goods and the din of their shouting was almost deafening. More than once the children found themselves pushed roughly aside as merchants and traders struggled beneath heavy loads.

As they neared the spot where the fishing boats lay moored, Varna pointed to a large group gathered around a man standing on an upturned hull. 'That's my father,' she announced. The children moved closer until they could make out what he was saying.

Several people in the crowd seemed to be hanging on his every word with worried expressions on their faces, while others laughed and some even started to jeer and heckle. 'Rubbish. Nonsense,' one of them shouted. 'Atlantis destroyed? Don't be daft. Are you crazy? You've been listening to spies like the ones who came here last year.' Medon carried on speaking over the jeers, but some people started to drift away shaking their heads in disbelief. However, a few stayed, eager to hear more. The children could see Medon was using all his powers of persuasion to try to convince them he was telling the truth. Then an anxious-looking man and woman who'd been hovering near the back of the crowd eased themselves further forward until they stood right in front of Medon.

'You've confirmed something which we already knew,' said the man. 'My wife's sister is blessed, or perhaps I should say cursed, with the gift of prophecy and for many years she's tried to convince people of the fate awaiting our nation. Nobody will listen to her and they say she's mad, but we believe her and we believe you. What can we do? How can we save ourselves?'

At once the others who'd stayed close to Medon started nodding and voicing their agreement. He began to speak, outlining the plans he'd made, and the power of his words soon held the attention of those who'd stayed behind to listen.

'He's doing okay isn't he?' said Varna proudly. 'Come on; let's go to the market.'

******

'All clear. Nobody home. They've all gone out, but the animal didn't seem to be with them.' A figure emerged from the shadow of a doorway facing Medon's house as the priest approached him.

'And you're sure the place is empty?'

'Yes, Master,' replied the temple attendant.

'Wait here and keep watch while I go inside,' said the priest. 'Hold this rattle and sound it if anyone comes back.' Handing over an odd-looking instrument, he disappeared through the curtained doorway into the house. Groping his way in the semi-darkness of the downstairs room, he peered into every corner and under the table. Nothing. He went upstairs to the bedroom and lifted the bedcovers one after another, desperately seeking his prey, but still couldn't find what he'd come for. Finally, he made his way up the stepladder on to the roof. A-ha, success at last.

The creature lay curled up asleep on a mattress, snoring fit to wake the dead. Taking out a canvas sack from under his robes, the priest threw it over the sleeping cat. Too late, Max awoke and, realising what was happening, started to struggle, but the man had already tied a cord around the neck of the sack which he swung across his shoulder before making his way back down the stepladder. Good grief, this animal weighed a ton.

'Jemima, help!' called Max, but his muffled cries went unheeded for there was no one to hear him.

******

If they'd thought the harbourside busy, they were totally

89

unprepared for the heaving mass of people crowding the market. Donkeys ferried goods from the port and the merchants drove them on in harsh voices, wielding sticks to encourage the over-laden animals. Anyone in their way was shouldered aside with no regard for their safety. It was all too much for Jemima who began to panic at the prospect of getting lost in the crush.

'Can we skirt around the edge, Varna?' she shouted, trying to make herself heard over the din.

'No problem,' replied Varna. 'It does seem busier than usual today, I must say. Follow me and we'll stay away from the middle.'

Sticking close to Varna they worked their way around one side of the marketplace until they arrived at an area where the crowd had thinned a little, allowing them to survey the scene properly.

'I was about to say it's like stepping back in time,' whispered Charlie, as he gazed around in amazement. 'But of course that's exactly what we've done.'

'Look at all the stalls selling just olives. I didn't realise they came in so many shapes, sizes and colours,' said Jemima.

'Varna, what's in those baskets full of different coloured powder and seeds?' asked Joe, pointing at a stall in front of them.

'They're spices,' she replied. 'You know, saffron, cumin, coriander ... and so on.' She raised her eyebrows, surprised he hadn't recognised something so obvious and exchanged a grin with Jemima.

Somewhat crestfallen, Joe kept quiet after that, too embarrassed to explain he thought spices came in small glass jars with printed labels to show what was in them.

Jemima noticed all the stalls had canvas signs suspended above them, bearing symbols advertising their wares. Some of the designs looked quite odd to her and, if the goods themselves hadn't been laid out on the trestle tables below, she would never have guessed what the pictures were meant to represent. The sign for the spice stall resembled a coffee pot and the fabric seller's sign showed an upright rectangle standing on three stick legs.

'Oh, there's my mother,' announced Varna and, following her pointing finger, they saw Aramina talking to a group of other women. Catching sight of the children she called them over.

'These children are our guests,' she explained, as she introduced Joe, Jemima and Charlie. 'It's all thanks to them that we're planning our new life in Kriti. Without their help who knows what might have happened to us.' The ladies

91

around Aramina smiled and nodded in greeting. 'Why don't you go back to the house now?' said Aramina. 'I'll come home and get lunch soon, but I've still got a few things to buy first. Will you take Simi with you? He's getting far too hot out here.' She handed the baby over to his sister.

'He's not the only one,' muttered Joe irritably. 'I'm roasting and I think the soles of my trainers might be melting.'

'Told you so,' said Jemima, making no attempt to conceal a smug grin as they set off back to the house.

# Chapter 12

'Max,' called Jemima, as they entered the house which felt blessedly cool after the heat outside. She received no answer, however, and a shiver of alarm ran down Jemima's spine. Glancing over to where she'd put the bowl of food for him that morning Jemima noticed it was untouched. It certainly wasn't like Max to ignore anything edible and she ran up the stairs with a growing sense of unease. Panting, she arrived on the roof terrace and, although she knew the search was futile, she hunted under every single blanket as the tears began to spill down her cheeks.

Joe and Charlie weren't far behind her.

'He's not here, Joe. He's gone,' she wailed. 'What's happened to him?'

Joe too was worried by Max's absence, but he attempted to calm Jemima down. 'He's probably wandered off to the loo, or gone to stretch his legs or something. He must have got bored because we've been out for such a long time.' Even to his own ears Joe knew he sounded rather unconvincing.

'He usually just sleeps when he's left by himself,' said Jemima. 'He hasn't touched his breakfast either.'

'Perhaps the weather's too hot for him,' replied Joe. 'He probably wasn't hungry or the food may have gone off in the heat. He's a sensible cat, Jemima, and he wouldn't go far without us. He'll be back, you'll see. Maybe he's met a nice lady cat in the neighbourhood.'

Jemima attempted a weak smile and did her best to put on a brave face, although the cold sensation in the pit of her stomach wouldn't go away.

'Sorry, I panicked,' she said. 'I just couldn't bear the thought of losing him.'

'I know,' answered Joe. 'Come on, let's go downstairs and help get lunch ready. Don't worry, Jem. I'm sure he'll turn up.'

Medon didn't return to join them for their meal, but while they ate Aramina happily told them about the success she'd had that morning. 'I've persuaded my sister, my friends and the neighbours on either side of here to come with us, as well as the parents of Mykos' friend Patros. I hope Medon is managing to convince people too.'

'He seemed to be doing all right when we were watching him,' said Varna. 'They're probably all busy sorting things out down at the harbour right now; there's going to be lots to organise.'

Lunch should have been a jolly affair as Aramina and Varna maintained a stream of excited chatter throughout the whole meal, discussing their forthcoming departure. Jemima, however, was extremely quiet and all she could think about was Max. She kept glancing over to the doorway, willing him to appear.

'It's so hot today,' said Aramina. 'You children should go down to the beach for a swim. We'll have plenty of time to finalise our plans when Medon gets back this evening.'

The boys readily agreed, but Jemima wasn't in the mood. She didn't want to stray too far from the house in case Max came back.

'You go,' she insisted. 'I don't feel like doing much this afternoon. I might try to find something I can use to make a picture of the temple and then I'll wander up there for a while.'

Aramina asked her what she meant, so Jemima explained that she wanted to draw the Temple of Poseidon as a souvenir to take home with them when they left.

'I might be able to think of something for you to use,' said Aramina. Varna had told her about Max's disappearance and the sight of Jemima's sad face touched her heart. 'You stay here, Jemima, and we'll see what we can find. The rest of

95

you can go now, if you're ready.'

The house was quiet again after Joe, Charlie, Varna and Mykos had left and Aramina put a drowsy Simi down on his bed for his afternoon nap. Then, taking Jemima by the hand, she led her over to a wooden coffer which stood against the wall and opened the lid to reveal its contents. The chest was full of all manner of odds and ends, scraps of material, assorted small clay pots and household items that Jemima couldn't identify. Aramina rummaged around in its depths for a moment before drawing out a length of white fabric.

'How about this?' she suggested, unfolding a piece of stiff, waxy cloth, a bit like tent canvas, which was roughly the size of a sheet of A3 paper. 'It's some old sailcloth from Medon's boat,' Aramina explained as Jemima ran her fingers over the material.

'Yes, I think that might work, but I'll need something to draw on it with.'

'Come upstairs, I've got an idea,' said Aramina.

She followed Varna's mother up the staircase leading to the bedroom where Aramina picked up a trinket box which she brought over to Jemima. The box contained a few simple pieces of carved wooden jewellery and some coloured beads. Jemima also spotted two small terracotta jars and what seemed to be a rather primitive thin paintbrush.

96

'I don't need these any more,' said Aramina, extracting the clay pots. 'I used to wear a little make-up on special occasions when I was younger, but I'm too old for that now and, besides, I no longer have the time with the children to look after. This one's got black in it for painting round my eyes and there's red in the other one for cheeks and lips.' She smiled at Jemima.

'You're beautiful, Aramina,' said Jemima. 'You don't need make-up. My Mum was the same.' As she spoke a sad look flitted across her face and Aramina stretched out a hand to touch Jemima's cheek.

'When you asked me about the strangers who came here before, Jemima, were those your parents?'

'We think so,' replied Jemima, trying her hardest not to cry. 'They've been missing for a while now and we've no idea where they are... but we're going to find them,' she added bravely. 'That's one of the reasons why we have to go home soon.'

'I'm sure you'll find them before long,' said Aramina, squeezing her hand. 'Now come on, let's go back downstairs and get some water to mix these powders with. Oh, and you'll also need this,' she added, picking up the small paintbrush.

Once they'd found a woven basket for Jemima to put

everything into, she kissed Aramina on the cheek and thanked her.

'Will you be all right by yourself?' asked Aramina.

'I'll be fine, thanks,' replied Jemima. 'Oh, and if Max comes home before I do would you please make sure he doesn't go out again?'

'Of course, and don't worry,' said Aramina. 'I expect he'll be waiting for you when you get back, but you won't stay out too long, will you?'

'No, I'll be back later,' answered Jemima as she ducked out through the door curtain and headed off up the lane, carrying her basket.

# Chapter 13

Jemima found a shady corner and sat down facing the grand building which dominated the square. The temple was an impressive sight and she doubted that her drawing skills would be able to do it justice. With care, however, she thought she might be able to produce something they could use as proof of their visit to Atlantis. Rummaging in the basket she took out the piece of cloth which she unfolded and laid flat on the ground before assembling her pots of paint and water. Not sure of where to begin she raised her head and began to study the building, unaware that as she gazed up at its exterior, another pair of eyes stared out from the interior studying her in return.

'Master, it's the girl, the one with the cat. She's outside in the square and behaving very oddly,' panted one of the temple attendants, gasping for breath after rushing to find the high priest.

'What exactly is she up to?'

'I'm not sure, Master. She's watching the temple,

muttering to herself and has arranged a variety of peculiar items on the ground in front of her. I think she may be casting a spell or a curse over us. Perhaps she knows we've got the animal, or maybe she's just spying on us. She ...'

'Stop babbling, man, for goodness sake and go and fetch the others,' spat the high priest. 'And make sure no one else is around outside when you grab her. The last thing we need is witnesses.'

Fortunately for Jemima, at that moment two ladies came out of their houses near to where she was sitting and began a lengthy conversation about the fabrics they'd seen down at the market earlier in the day. One of them had a daughter's wedding to prepare for and so had plenty to say. They chattered on for ages and Jemima listened with half an ear, humming softly to herself while she worked on her picture. The sketch seemed to be coming along rather well she thought, as she leaned back and admired her efforts. An hour went by, during which time the sun had moved round in the sky and was now shining on what had been Jemima's shady spot.

She'd just about finished and decided to call it a day. She only had to complete the complicated symbols representing Poseidon's name in the rectangle beneath his image and she concentrated hard to make sure she copied them as accurately as possible. The two ladies had gone their separate ways by now and all was quiet again in the square. As Jemima was packing away her belongings into the basket she became aware of a shadow looming over her and she sat up with a start.

'Good afternoon, young lady.'

She raised her head, squinting against the sun. A man in long blue robes stood before her and Jemima thought he looked very strange. She saw he was wearing make-up; thick, black, sweeping lines ringed his eyelids, giving him a rather theatrical appearance. He was also completely bald and the fierce rays of the sun reflected off his shiny head, creating the effect of a halo.

'Goodness, you made me jump,' answered Jemima, a little taken aback.

'Please accept my sincere apologies, Miss,' he said in an oily voice. 'That wasn't my intention, I do assure you.' He attempted a smile which didn't quite reach his eyes. 'I've been watching you and am merely interested in what you're doing.'

'Oh,' said Jemima. 'I was painting a picture of the temple because it's so beautiful...' She realised as she spoke that the man might be angry with her. She hadn't asked permission to draw the sacred building and perhaps such things weren't allowed.

'How lovely!' he exclaimed. 'May I see?'

Jemima breathed a sigh of relief and took the piece of material out of the basket, holding it up in front of him.

'Excellent,' he said, barely even glancing at her painting. 'You must come and show this fine piece of work to the high priest. He would be most honoured by the respect you have bestowed upon our temple.'

'I'm not sure,' answered Jemima. 'I ought to be getting back.' She hesitated, remembering all the warnings about not speaking to strangers.

'Just for a moment,' he insisted. 'It won't take long.'

Jemima thought for a minute. Actually, it would be quite interesting to see *inside* the temple. According to Varna, ordinary people never got the chance and she'd be able to tell her all about it afterwards ... and Joe would be really jealous too.

'All right, but I can't stay long,' she said. 'They're expecting me home soon.'

She grabbed her basket and followed the priest up the flight of steps into the temple. At first she couldn't focus on a single thing after coming in from the bright sunlit square, but her pupils soon adjusted to the subdued glow given off by the many oil lamps which adorned the dark interior and she became aware of a tall figure approaching her. Just like the priest who'd first spoken to her, he too was dressed in royal blue robes and wore dramatic black eyeliner. Unlike the other priest, however, he wasn't bald; his shoulder-length black hair looked suspiciously like a wig and perched on top of his head he wore some sort of gold headdress, similar to a tiara. He reminded Jemima of a pantomime villain and she almost let out a nervous giggle which mercifully stuck in her throat when she noticed him glaring at her with eyes as cold as ice.

She bowed her head, trying to appear respectful as she scrabbled in her basket for the piece of material with a trembling hand. Holding out her picture she began to speak in a quavering voice. 'I've brought my drawing to......' She didn't get a chance to finish the sentence.

'Silence, girl,' he bellowed. 'How dare you address me, the high priest, in this sacred place?' He signalled to the other priests and attendants behind him. 'Take her to join her companion.'

They immediately sprang to do his bidding and Jemima found herself surrounded. In her fright she dropped the basket, but managed to cling on to the square of sailcloth which she still held clenched in her right hand.

Then everything went dark as a large sheet of material

103

was flung over her head. Terrified, she wondered where on earth they were taking her and why? How would anyone ever find her? They bundled her into something that felt like a big sack before lifting her off the ground and carrying her away. Too shocked even to call out for help, she lay stunned inside the scratchy canvas while they bumped her along to goodness knows where.

After a short while she heard a metallic grating noise, followed by the loud creaking of hinges in need of a good oiling. The next moment she landed with a thump on the floor and the sack was whisked roughly off her.

'There, you've got company. Aren't you lucky?' announced a sneering voice.

A nasty cackle echoed in her ears before the door banged shut again, leaving her sitting on a hard floor in the pitch darkness. Tears began to roll down her cheeks and a sob forced its way out of her mouth. Suddenly, to her horror, something furry brushed against her hand.

*Oh no, rats.* She shuddered and sprang to her feet with a scream of terror. Then she heard a familiar voice.

'It's me, Jemima. Thank goodness you're here.'

'Max, oh Max, you're all right,' she sobbed and fell to her knees, reaching out for his warm body. Grabbing hold of the large cat, she hugged him to her, shedding hot tears into his silky coat.

After a while he grunted, 'Could you squeeze me a little less tightly, do you think? I do have to breathe, you know.'

Jemima released her grip slightly.

'What on earth's going on, Max? Why are we here?'

'I'm not sure,' he replied. 'I knew there was something evil in that temple right from the start and unfortunately it seems as if I've been proved right. The important thing now is to find a way out of this place.'

# Chapter 14

'Isn't Jemima back yet?' asked Joe when they all returned from the beach.

'No,' answered Aramina, who was in the middle of preparing the evening meal. 'And to tell you the truth, I'm starting to get a little worried. She told me she wouldn't be long.'

'We'll go and find her,' said Joe. 'I expect she's lost track of the time. Either that or she's gone off looking for Max.'

'Well, please fetch her back because dinner will be ready soon,' replied Aramina.

Joe and Charlie went outside and set off towards the temple. On arriving in the square, however, there was absolutely no sign of Jemima.

'Where on earth has she got to?' Joe muttered crossly. Tramping about the city looking for his sister was the last thing he felt like doing right now. They wandered on, peering up alleyways and down side streets as far as the palace, but still couldn't find her.

'This isn't like Jemima,' said Joe, as a niggle of doubt started to creep into his mind. 'She wouldn't wander off; she's too much of a goody-goody.'

'We ought to go home and tell Aramina,' suggested Charlie.

The two boys raced back to the house and arrived panting for breath.

Aramina looked up expectantly as they came in.

'Where's Jemima?' she asked.

'We don't know,' said Joe and his lower lip trembled as the seriousness of the situation began to sink in. They had to find Jemima ... and soon. Returning to their own time was impossible without her and he dreaded to think what would happen if they didn't find her before the disaster struck Atlantis.

Aramina sank down on to the bench by the table, anxiety washing over her. She'd become so attached to these children since they'd come to stay and she felt sick with worry at the prospect of anything happening to Jemima.

'Medon will be home soon,' she said. 'He'll know what to do.'

When her husband arrived Aramina hurriedly explained the situation and he left the house again straightaway, promising to find Jemima and bring her back. Meanwhile

Aramina insisted they should sit down and eat, but the general atmosphere of worry meant no one had much of an appetite. Medon returned several hours later ... alone.

'I asked all the neighbours if anyone had seen her,' he told Aramina. 'I also bumped into your friend Klymene who told me she'd spotted Jemima in the square earlier. Klymene was talking to the wife of Almenides the baker for almost an hour and Jemima was sitting near the temple all that time. Then the ladies went their separate ways, but Jemima had gone when Klymene came back later.'

'First Max and now Jemima,' said Joe worriedly. 'Where are they?'

'We'll find them, Joe,' answered Varna. 'They can't have gone far.'

\*\*\*\*\*\*

Medon and Aramina talked late into the night, sharing their concern for Jemima and discussing the preparations for leaving Atlantis. 'My sister Delphina says her lot will all come with us,' said Aramina. 'The neighbours either side of us too, and also the family of Mykos' friend Patros from up the street. Two of my other friends are going to try and persuade their husbands this evening. How did you get on?'

'Not badly,' replied Medon. 'Obviously, my brother Delon will come, as well as three other fishermen and their families too.' He also told her about the couple who'd approached him at the end of his speech. 'We'll be able to use our own boats and I spoke to a merchant from Kriti who says he's more than happy to take anyone without their own transport, for a price of course.'

'I can't even think of going anywhere while that poor child's missing though,' said Aramina.

'Don't fret, my love, we'll find her,' replied Medon, in what he hoped was a reassuring voice. 'Come on, let's go and get some rest. We've got a lot to do tomorrow.'

Nobody, however, slept particularly well that night. They spent the hours of darkness imagining all sorts of horrors and it was a relief for everyone when dawn finally broke.

\*\*\*\*\*\*

The family weren't the only ones who'd been unable to sleep. Jemima and Max had struggled to get comfortable in the confined cell and with no furniture they'd just had to huddle together on the floor, but at least it wasn't cold. They spent the whole night worrying about their fate and whether the

109

others would find them before it was too late – too late for what, Jemima didn't want to even think about. Early the following morning the door opened briefly and a hand thrust something in through the gap. Jemima couldn't see who the hand belonged to as she was dazzled by the unaccustomed light bursting through the open doorway, after spending so many hours in complete darkness.

'Take this and be thankful you're being fed,' growled a harsh voice. 'You're getting better treatment than most prisoners do.'

They'd been given a jug of water, a hunk of bread and a bowl full of an unidentifiable sloppy substance which smelled revolting. Nevertheless, having had nothing since the previous day, the two captives both ate hungrily, not knowing when their next meal might be. Jemima cupped her hand and poured some water into it for Max to drink before taking a long swig from the jug herself.

'I think we must be in that condemned prisoners' cell we passed the other day,' said Jemima after the door had slammed shut. 'Serves me right for wondering what it was like inside. I wish I didn't know now.'

'Well, there's no window in here,' replied Max. 'So the only way in and out is through the door. Perhaps the next time they open it one of us should try and escape. It might be easier for me to have a go, but that would mean leaving you by yourself, Jemima. What do you think?'

'Sounds like a good plan, Max. If you can fetch help I'll be okay on my own for a while,' said Jemima bravely, although in truth the prospect of remaining in this ghastly place all alone filled her with absolute dread.

# Chapter 15

Medon left the house early to embark on a thorough search of Atlantis, asking anyone he met if they'd seen Jemima. No one had, but everyone promised to keep an eye out for her.

Throughout the morning official proclamations were made throughout the whole city by two priests, accompanied by a fanfare of trumpets to ensure no one should miss the important news.

'This afternoon a special ceremony is being held at the temple, including the sacrifice of a sacred bull,' they announced. 'Poseidon is angry and must be appeased, so all citizens are to attend. The rites will begin at the fourth hour after noon.'

Today was even hotter than the day before and the air felt sticky and oppressive. Everyone seemed on edge, partly owing to the excessive heat and also because they'd been unsettled by Medon's warnings from the previous day. Of course, rumours had spread like wildfire and, as in a game of

Chinese whispers, the facts had changed so much that no one knew what was true any more. The city streets buzzed with tales of spies, plots and the destruction of Atlantis, and people glanced nervously over their shoulders as they spoke. Now, to add to the sense of unease, an unexpected special ceremony at the temple had been announced. This wasn't a feast day or a holiday, so it could only mean bad news.

Suddenly the echo of a distant rumble was heard and for a moment the earth quivered like a jelly. Then, almost as quickly, everything returned to normal once again. This just made the general mood in the town worse and many of the inhabitants felt even more anxious than before.

'The priests were right,' said one man. 'Poseidon *does* seem to be angry.'

'Yes,' added another. 'Did you feel his horses stamping their hooves in rage just then? I'd say he's hopping mad about something.'

Everyone was now convinced of the importance of attending the temple ceremony and all agreed they would have to make many offerings to calm the sea god's fury.

Joe, Charlie, Varna and Mykos spent a fruitless morning hunting for Jemima and soon ran out of places to search. By now Joe was in despair.

'I wish we'd never set foot in Atlantis,' he wailed. 'This is all my fault. She didn't want to come here and I made her.'

'Don't give up, Joe,' said Charlie, trying to reassure him, although he too had been having similar thoughts. 'I know we'll find her – after all she can't be far away in a place this size.'

The family met up again back at the house, where Aramina had spent the morning fretting about Jemima's whereabouts. Over lunch, Medon impressed upon them the necessity of their attendance at the temple that afternoon.

'We can ask for Poseidon's help in finding Jemima. If we make an offering to him I'm sure he'll listen to our prayers.'

Secretly Joe and Charlie were rather unconvinced by this, but had reached the stage where anything was worth a try.

So later that afternoon the boys found themselves being swept along by the surging crowds which filled the tiny street leading up to the square. They tried to stick close to the family, but this proved to be impossible in the heaving mass of people and they soon became separated from Medon and the others. Eventually as the crowd wound its way up the hill Joe and Charlie ended up in the middle of the square.

'It's so hot I can hardly breathe,' gasped Charlie. He'd heard enough stories about people getting crushed underfoot by big crowds in confined spaces and he fought to keep down a rising tide of panic.

'Hang on to me,' said Joe. 'I'll try and work my way to the edge of the square – there'll probably be a bit more breathing space over there.'

He began to shuffle between the rows of people, slowly inching his way forwards. In spite of much grumbling and receiving a few sharp elbows in his ribs, Joe persevered until they finally found themselves on the fringes of the crowd.

'You can let go of my tee shirt now, Charlie,' he said, breathing a sigh of relief.

No sooner had they taken up their position than a deafening blare of trumpets sounded and two priests dressed in bright blue robes came out of the temple, followed by six attendants.

'Make way for the High Priest Zorotes,' announced one of the robed men.

Then, to the accompaniment of another fanfare, a tall, regal figure emerged and began to descend the steps. The crowd fell silent, bowing their heads in reverence. Zorotes too wore rich blue robes and was adorned in a dazzling array of gold jewellery, including a shining diadem which sat on his head of flowing black hair. Joe sneaked a quick look at him and decided he didn't like what he saw. The priest had a thin, cruel mouth and snakelike, glittering eyes.

115

'Citizens of Atlantis,' pronounced Zorotes in a loud voice. 'Lord Poseidon has commanded your presence here today. He is extremely angered by the events of these last few days, for it has come to his attention that strangers have arrived in our midst, intent on stirring up trouble. Worse still, they have even persuaded some gullible people to forget their loyalty to him and to consider abandoning Atlantis altogether. Such scandalous talk must cease at once and all wicked plans cast aside or Poseidon himself will punish everyone in our city for these crimes. As for the strangers, they shall be dealt with accordingly.'

Joe and Charlie exchanged worried looks. What strangers? Was he referring to them?

'Do you think this might have something to do with Jemima's disappearance?' asked Joe, feeling a little sick.

'I hope not,' answered Charlie, his knees knocking together.

'... And so,' continued the high priest in a booming voice, 'Today we will offer a special sacrifice to Poseidon to confirm our loyalty and devotion to him.'

He turned and clapped his hands, at which two more temple attendants appeared from around the side of the building, leading a large bull with garlands of white flowers draped round its neck. The huge animal looked incredibly

116

strong and the young men seemed to be having difficulty controlling it.

'Crikey,' said Charlie. 'I hope that thing doesn't break loose. We're so packed in here no one would have any chance of running away from it.'

At last the men succeeded in dragging the bull to the stone altar which stood at the base of the steps in front of the temple. Once more the high priest began to speak. 'Mighty Poseidon, accept this gift from the faithful people of Atlantis. Calm your anger and forgive our sins, we humbly beseech you.'

As he spoke Joe and Charlie glanced up just in time to see a shining flash of metal as the priest swung a dagger through the air, plunging it deep into the bull's neck. The creature bellowed and its front legs started to wobble, before it sank to its knees. The two other priests rushed forward and began to collect the blood in golden bowls as the hot crimson liquid spurted from the wide slash in its throat.

'Oh yuck, that's horrible,' said Joe, aghast, looking sideways at Charlie who'd turned an interesting shade of green.

The crowd roared and cheered as the bull slowly grew weaker before collapsing on the ground. Next, the temple attendants darted forward with flaming torches and touched them to the pile of tinder-dry wood which had been stacked up like a bonfire next to the altar, causing leaping tongues of fire to shoot skywards.

'As if it's not hot enough already,' moaned Charlie.

More attendants approached bearing pitchers of dark-red wine, half of which they poured into the bowls containing the sacrificial blood. The remainder was used to fill golden goblets which were handed out to all the priests who drank deeply from them.

'All right for some,' muttered someone behind Joe.

Each priest then stepped forward in turn, pouring a small quantity of wine on to the flames, followed by the attendants who emptied the bowls containing the blood over the fire as the high priest raised his hands to the sky, his eyes closed in prayer.

'Lord Poseidon, we dedicate this sacred bull to you. Please accept our sacrifice.'

At the word "sacrifice" a rumbling sound came from beneath everyone's feet and again the earth shook. For a moment or two, it was as if solid ground had turned to water and the priest's eyes snapped open in alarm.

'He is still not satisfied and it may be too late to change his mind now. Beware the wrath of Poseidon, citizens of Atlantis!'

Angrily turning on his heel he swept back up the steps and disappeared into the hallowed precincts of the temple, leaving his fellow priests and the attendants to clear away the debris left behind after the sacrifice, including the carcass of the bull which should have been burnt on the altar, had Zorotes not cut the ceremony short. A loud muttering came from the uneasy crowd, soon rising into a crescendo of anxious cries as they started to disperse in all directions like a herd of panicked animals.

Joe and Charlie, still rather shell-shocked by the gruesome spectacle they'd just witnessed, remained rooted to the spot and sat down on the ground, their trembling legs unable to hold them upright any longer.

'I don't ever want to see anything like that again,' said Joe, utterly sickened by the whole scene.

'I agree,' replied Charlie. 'My parents took me to a bullfight once when we were on holiday in Spain and I thought that was bad enough – I kept my hands over my face practically all the way through – but this was far worse.'

One of the temple attendants who'd been left to clear up the mess overheard their conversation. His eyes combed the rapidly-emptying square, before swivelling back to study the two boys. Then he turned to mount the steps in an unhurried manner, trying not to draw attention to himself,

119

but once inside dashed off to find the high priest.

'Master, the other two strangers, the boys, are here. They witnessed the sacrifice and are still out in the square discussing it.'

'You know what must be done,' replied Zorotes with a sly smile. 'Fetch the others to help you.'

# Chapter 16

Joe and Charlie remained seated in the corner of the square for a few minutes longer until their trembling legs had recovered enough to allow them to move. They stood up somewhat shakily and were surprised to find themselves surrounded by the priests and attendants who, a few moments previously, had been clearing up after the ceremony.

'You're coming with us,' announced one of the priests, his shiny, bald head illuminated by the sun.

Joe and Charlie had no say in the matter and were completely hidden from view by the encircling wall of men who frogmarched them into the temple.

'I did say I wanted a look inside,' Joe whispered through the side of his mouth, in an attempt to sound braver than he felt.

'Silence, insolent boy,' shouted one of the priests, prodding him forward.

The men pushed them into a chamber just off the large

entrance hall and, passing through the open space, Joe and Charlie noticed a huge statue of the god Poseidon. Painted in bright colours, it made him appear eerily lifelike. They didn't have time to take in their surroundings though, as the priests hustled the two boys along, not allowing them to pause for a second. At last they drew to a halt, finding themselves in front of the high priest in all his grandeur. Up close, he seemed even taller than he had outside and the boys cowered before him, feeling very small in comparison.

'So now I have the full set,' sneered Zorotes. 'You thought you'd be able to get away with coming to our land and stirring up unrest. Well, you'll soon find out what we do to spies.'

He put a hand inside his robes, drawing out a large key which hung on a leather cord around his neck and he handed it to the bald-headed priest.

'Here, take these specimens to join the others,' he commanded, waving them away with a dismissive gesture.

Two of the attendants had already been sent outside to check the coast was clear and they returned, nodding their heads.

'No one's about. Everywhere's deserted.'

Once more surrounded by a wall of priests Joe and Charlie were marched quickly out through the back entrance of the temple and up the street. The men stopped in front of the small prison and Joe gulped. What now, he wondered?

Inside the cell Jemima and Max had heard the approaching footsteps and the voices, one of which they recognised as the priest with the bald head.

'Get ready, Max,' said Jemima. 'This might be our only chance.'

A grating noise signalled the turning of the key in the lock and then the door was pushed open. As Joe and Charlie were shoved unceremoniously through the entrance Max sprang forward and shot out between the forest of legs. He hurtled off along the street as fast as his paws would carry him, not daring to slow down and look back.

'Blast!' cursed the bald priest. 'Now we'll have to waste time hunting for him all over again. In the meantime, best not mention anything to Zorotes about our little setback. We don't need to make him even angrier, do we?' They slammed the door shut and turned the key in the lock once more.

It was pitch black inside and the boys couldn't see a thing.

'Joe? Charlie?' A tiny, quavering voice came from the far corner of the cell.

'Jemima, is that you?' ventured Joe. 'Oh thank goodness.

123

Everyone's been so worried about you. Were you locked in here all this time?'

'Yes, and you can't imagine how vile it's been,' she wailed, promptly bursting into tears.

'Don't worry,' he said, crawling over to where she sat and grabbing hold of her hand. 'We're here now and we'll find a way to get ourselves out, won't we, Charlie?'

'Er ... yes, I suppose so,' answered Charlie, a touch uncertainly. 'Hey Jemima, was that Max who ran past as they chucked us inside?'

'Yes,' said Jemima. 'I found him here when I arrived. The priests snatched him from the house on the day we all went to the market. Anyway, we planned his escape and it's worked. I just hope they don't manage to catch him again because he's gone to fetch help. He knows what to do and thank goodness he can talk now – that's if he can find someone who'll listen to him.'

# Chapter 17

Max ran flat out. Galloping all the way back down the street to Medon's house he screeched through the open doorway at high speed and a startled Varna turned round to look as his claws skidded to a halt on the stone floor. The exhausted cat was puffing and panting for all he was worth, unused to such strenuous exercise. Varna had been alone in the house wondering what she should do. Both her parents were still out making preparations for their forthcoming departure and she was waiting for the boys to come home. No one had seen hide nor hair of them since the ceremony at the temple – they should have returned ages ago.

'Oh, Max.' She jumped up and ran over to the gasping cat, picking him up for a cuddle. 'Thank goodness. Everyone's been worried sick about you and Jemima will be so glad you're back – or at least she would be if she was here. We don't know where she is,' she said sadly.

'I do,' answered Max.

Varna screamed and promptly dropped him on the floor.

'Careful,' he said, giving her an admonishing glance as he picked himself up. 'That hurt, you know.'

She stared at Max, her eyes as wide as saucers. She couldn't believe her ears. Was she imagining things or did he just speak? She must have spent too long out in the sun today, she thought, shaking all over.

'Varna, you must listen to me,' he said, gazing into her eyes.

She gasped. He really had spoken; she saw his lips move.

'H-how c-can y-you t-talk?' she stammered in disbelief. This wasn't right. A cat shouldn't be able to speak. Only some sort of dark magic or an evil spirit could cause such a thing to happen. No, her mind had to be playing tricks on her.

'Varna, please, there may not be a lot of time. We must hurry,' insisted Max.

Varna collapsed on to the bench by the table, her legs trembling so much she couldn't stand up any longer.

'They've got Jemima, and now they've taken Joe and Charlie too. I managed to escape,' he continued breathlessly.

On hearing their names Varna was finally convinced that she wasn't imagining things and, although this was still way beyond her comprehension, she took a deep breath and answered him.

'Who's got them?' she asked. It felt weird talking to a cat, knowing the animal understood and would answer.

'The priests,' explained Max. 'First I was kidnapped on the day you were all out, then they snatched Jemima while she was drawing the temple and now Joe and Charlie have been captured as well. I managed to get away when they opened the door to put them in with us.'

'But where are they and why would the priests want to kidnap you all?' asked Varna. 'That doesn't make any sense.'

'We were all put in that prison cell opposite the Law Court,' replied Max. 'The priests think we're spies and you told us spies used to be executed. We've got to rescue the children before they do something horrible to them.'

Varna was stunned. It might be true, she supposed, but how on earth could she solve a problem like this? She wished her parents would hurry up and come home. 'My father will know what to do,' she said. 'When he gets back ...'

'We can't wait till then,' Max interrupted her. 'He might not be back for ages.'

'But how can we get them out?' she asked. 'Surely the priests will be guarding the cell, won't they?'

'I don't think so, but the door's locked.'

'Well, we can't force open a locked door,' said Varna. 'We're going to need help.'

'No time,' panted Max, already on his way out of the house. 'Come on, Varna, we must try something.'

Varna scrambled to her feet and ran through the doorway after him. *By Zeus, what a bossy cat!*

Once outside, however, Max realised that perhaps it might not be a good idea for him to be seen in the street. The priests were bound to be looking for him right now and he wouldn't be any use to the children if he was recaptured. He stopped dead and did an about-turn, running back into the house, leaving Varna wondering what on earth was going on. She followed him inside again.

'Change of plan,' he stated. 'I forgot I'm a wanted cat at the moment, being on the run and so on. I'll need to travel incognito.'

Varna looked totally baffled, so he explained his predicament.

'Ah,' she said. 'I'll go and find you a disguise.' She thought for a moment before disappearing upstairs.

'Hurry up, Varna,' called Max. 'We haven't got all day.'

'All right,' she huffed. 'I'm coming.' She ran back down the staircase with a bundle of material in her arms. 'Simi's baby clothes from when he was younger,' she explained, as she knelt on the floor and began wrapping Max in what felt like yards of fabric.

'Not so tight,' he groaned. 'It would be quite useful if I could breathe.'

When Varna was at last convinced he resembled an infant rather than a cat she picked him up and carried him out of the house.

'Now act normally,' whispered Max. 'Pretend you're out for a pleasant stroll with the cute little baby.'

*Jolly heavy baby, and not so little*, thought Varna, her arms beginning to ache already.

They walked on up the street and Varna kept her head down, trying to appear inconspicuous. On reaching the square she scuttled through as fast as possible, but fortunately there didn't seem to be anyone around. Breathing a sigh of relief she hurried onwards, but just then two of the temple attendants emerged from an alley and Varna almost dropped Max in terror.

'Waaah,' he wailed, in what he hoped was a convincing attempt at a baby's cry.

'Shh,' said Varna, scared stiff in case the men heard.

Luckily the two attendants took no notice whatsoever and turned down the street towards the square. Varna continued on her way until she arrived at the Law Court. Glancing furtively around, she made sure nobody was watching and, hoisting Max on to her shoulder, ambled over to the prison cell opposite.

'Jemima, are you in there?' she called in a hoarse whisper.

'Varna, is that you?' answered Jemima with a cry of relief.

'Yes, and Max is here too,' replied Varna. 'Why didn't you warn me he could talk? He almost frightened me to death.'

'We weren't sure you'd understand,' said Joe. 'Listen, Varna, please try and get us out of here. We don't know how long we've got until the priests come back for us.'

'But how? The door's locked.'

'When they took us into the temple, the high priest had the key on a cord around his neck,' said Joe. 'Somehow you're going to have to get hold of that key.'

'Oh fine,' she retorted. 'I'll just go up to him and ask to borrow it, shall I?'

'We'll find a way,' said Max. 'I'm sure we'll think of something.'

'Well don't take too long,' replied Joe. 'We need to get out of here as soon as we can.'

'Oh Max, you've been brilliant,' added Jemima. 'I'm so proud of you and I know you won't let us down. I can't wait to give you a great big hug when we get out of here.'

'You might change your mind if you saw what I look like at the moment,' muttered the large cat, rather embarrassed by his disguise.

'What did you say?' asked Jemima.

'Nothing important,' he sighed. 'Sit tight and I'm sure we'll get you out of there in no time.'

'We'd better go,' said Varna. 'We don't want to draw attention to ourselves. We'll try and find a way of getting the key somehow.'

'Please do your best,' urged Joe.

Varna and her "baby" slipped away from the door of the prison, racking their brains for a plan of action as they hurried home.

'I've had a thought,' said Max. 'Whoever takes the food to the cell also has a key. I wonder if it's the same one and whether they take it back to the high priest afterwards.'

'That's a good point,' replied Varna. 'But I still don't see how *we're* going to get hold of the key, no matter who has it.'

As they approached the house Varna's parents appeared in the doorway.

'Ah Varna, there you are,' said Aramina. 'I'm going to need your help. We've had a meeting with all the people concerned and everyone still wants to go ahead with our departure, in spite of the priest's warnings this afternoon.

131

We've got to start packing straightaway as we need to be ready to leave the day after tomorrow. First of all I'd like you to ...' She stopped mid-sentence as her eyes lit upon Max. 'Oh, the cat's back.'

'Yes, and you'll never guess what,' began Varna. 'He ...'

Suddenly she caught sight of Max furiously shaking his head from side to side and realised at once that he was trying to tell her to stop. Yes, perhaps he was right and it would be better not to mention talking cats in front of grown-ups.

'Yes? He what?' asked Aramina, waiting impatiently for Varna to finish.

'He, er, he ... he wasn't missing after all. He'd been round at one of the neighbour's houses... they've got a female cat,' she finished lamely. Max looked daggers at her as she added this last bit and she could swear he was blushing.

'Well, at least he's here now,' said Aramina. 'What about poor little Jemima? Any news?'

Varna glanced across at Max for help, but he was simply nodding.

'Um, she's fine,' mumbled Varna. 'She'd got lost, but Joe found her and they'll all be back soon. They've just gone to do a last bit of sight-seeing.'

'Oh, thank goodness,' said Aramina with a heartfelt sigh

of relief. 'But where on earth did she sleep, out there all alone by herself? I shall have a few words to say to her when she gets back though. Fancy going off and worrying us all like that... and she must be starving, the poor scrap! She hasn't had anything to eat since yesterday lunchtime. And what ...?'

'Stop worrying, Mother. She's fine,' repeated Varna. 'There's really no need to make such a fuss. Jemima will explain everything when she gets back.'

'Well, if you're sure she's all right,' said Aramina uncertainly. She took a deep breath, thankful that Jemima was safe, and prepared to focus once more on organising the packing. 'Will you go upstairs, Varna, and make a start on sorting out things we need to take with us? Put anything we can get rid of to one side and while you're doing that I'll get us something to eat.'

Varna mounted the stairs while Max followed closely behind.

'What did you say that for?' he growled crossly. 'The bit about the girl cat.'

'I don't know. It was the first thing that came into my head,' replied Varna as she attempted to stifle a giggle.

Up in the bedroom Varna started sorting through piles of clothes and linens which were stored in a large wooden chest.

'Anyway,' continued Max. 'Back to the matter in hand. We'd better decide how we're going to rescue the others. It'll have to be tonight: we daren't leave it until tomorrow and besides, I don't want them spending any more time than is absolutely necessary in that horrible place.'

'How on earth are we going to get the key off Zorotes though?' asked Varna. 'Should we try to intercept the priests when they take food to the cell?'

'Varna? Are you talking to yourself up there?' called Aramina from downstairs. 'Please get on with what you're supposed to be doing.'

'Yes, Mother.'

In a quieter voice Max made a few suggestions. 'Let's start by following the priests who bring the food to the cell, then we can watch what happens to the key afterwards. If they take it back to the high priest we'll have to try stealing it off him when he's asleep tonight.'

'And how do you suggest we manage to do all that without being spotted?' asked Varna. 'We're hardly invisible, are we?'

'Hmm, I haven't finished working out the finer details. Just give me a few moments.' Half an hour later he was still pondering the problem, when Aramina called Varna to come and eat. Max was also given a bowl of tasty morsels which he wolfed down, ravenous after his meagre rations in prison.

'I need to go out for a little while this evening, if that's okay?' said Varna. 'I'm meeting the others and then we'll all come home together afterwards.'

'All right,' replied Medon. 'But make sure you're not out too long because your mother needs you to help her and we'll all have to get up early in the morning. Tomorrow will be our last day here and there's still lots to do.'

'Yes, Father. I won't be back late.'

After bolting down their food as quickly as possible Varna and Max scooted up to the roof terrace to finalise the rescue plans.

'Just one thing,' said Max with a sniff. 'I'm not dressing up as a baby again. It was most undignified.'

\*\*\*\*\*\*

A little while later Varna left the house bearing a large basket covered with a cloth. By Zeus, this was even heavier than carrying him like a baby, she thought. She trudged up the lane, slowly making her way towards the prison. Turning into a side alley near to the cell, she sat on a doorstep and plonked her heavy burden on the ground beside her.

'Oi, put me down a bit more gently next time, would you?' cried a muffled voice.

'Shh,' hissed Varna, as she settled down to wait.

'Anything yet?' he asked a few moments later.

'No, not yet.'

Thirty seconds passed. 'Still nothing?' came a plaintive whine from within the basket.

'No. Now be quiet. Someone might hear you.'

Ten more minutes went by and even Varna was starting to get bored when she heard the sound of approaching footsteps. She risked peeping round the corner of the alley and, sure enough, two priests had stopped outside the cell. One of them produced a key hanging on a leather cord with which he unlocked the door while the other one thrust a jug and a bowl of food inside. They slammed the door shut again after making a few nasty remarks to the prisoners and set off back down the street.

Varna grabbed hold of the basket and, hoisting it on to her hip, began to follow them at a safe distance, being careful to make as little noise as possible. The priests disappeared through the rear door of the temple and so she stopped at the corner of the square, bending to put her burden down – remembering to do it a bit more carefully this time. Before she'd even had chance to straighten up

136

again she was startled by a sudden movement as Max leapt out of the basket and shot into the building behind the two men.

'No, Max,' cried Varna. 'Come back. Oh, please be careful.'

He disappeared from sight, leaving Varna outside wondering what on earth she should do now. She sat down to wait, anxiously biting her nails.

# Chapter 18

Once inside, Max looked around him. The place seemed empty, but he didn't want to risk being spotted so he kept to the shadows. Slinking along the walls of the large chamber, he wondered where the two priests had gone. Several doorways led out of the room, but he was unsure which to try first. As he considered his options he became aware of the sound of approaching voices and in a panic hunted around for somewhere to hide. He made a hasty dive for cover behind a large statue just as the two priests came back into the room, laughing and joking.

'Hah! Those spies are for it,' laughed one of the men. 'Zorotes says he's already decided how to get rid of them.'

'I hope we can find that wretched cat again before Zorotes knows the creature's missing,' replied the other one. 'Otherwise we'll be for it as well.'

Max's fur bristled and he jolly well hoped they *would* suffer the wrath of Zorotes; they deserved it. The priests crossed the room before disappearing through another doorway and as the sound of their footsteps faded into the distance Max cautiously emerged from his hiding place.

'Just one moment,' hissed a quiet voice. 'Who are you and where do you think you're going?'

Max stopped in his tracks and found himself staring into a pair of almond-shaped eyes of bright emerald green. He cleared his throat but, unusually for him, seemed to be lost for words.

'Well, I'm waiting...' said the voice. 'Come out and show yourself.' Max stepped nervously forward. Standing before him was one of the most beautiful cats he'd ever seen. She looked him up and down in a rather haughty manner. 'What's the matter?' she asked. 'Has a person got your tongue?'

'I ...er.... um ...no ...I....,' he stammered.

'Spit it out for goodness sake. You're starting to bore me.'

Max took a deep breath, deciding he had no choice but to tell her everything. 'I'm sorry,' he replied. 'You startled me. Do you think we could discuss this somewhere a bit more private? I don't want anyone else overhearing us.'

She paused for a moment, her head on one side, studying him carefully as she considered his request. Then she seemed to make up her mind and nodded, before leading him over to a shadowy corner of the room. He followed on trembling legs. They both sat down and Max began to speak, telling his story as quickly as possible. He knew he was taking a risk and that she could denounce him to the priests at any moment, but he had no alternative. She let him tell his tale from start to finish, however, giving little mews of encouragement every now and again.

'You're a brave cat, Max,' she murmured, flashing an admiring smile in his direction when he'd finished speaking.

He puffed out his chest in pride, although he did his best to appear modest. 'Oh no, I'm sure any cat would do the same under the circumstances,' he said. 'And besides I'd willingly risk my own life to save those children, especially my Jemima.'

'Well, I'm going to help you,' she answered. 'My name's Mia and I'm the temple cat here. You'd never believe half the things I've seen in this place. Zorotes, the high priest, is a horrid, cruel man and I can imagine only too well how badly he's treated your friends. He's always kicking me when he thinks no one's looking and he laughs if it makes me howl in pain, ignoring the fact that I'm supposed to be revered and respected. Now, after what you've told me about the fate of Atlantis, I don't want to stay here and I've certainly no intention of spending my last moments in the company of

Zorotes. In fact I can't imagine anything worse. Can I come with you when you go?'

Max soon realised that his first impressions of Mia as cold and haughty had been wrong. She sounded keen to help him rescue the children and, in return, Max felt proud that he could save her from her unhappy life in the temple. In all honesty he was more than a little dazzled by her beauty and found her sleek, dark, aristocratic looks quite bewitching, especially those stunning green eyes and her glossy fur the colour of bitter chocolate. He didn't realise that she, in turn, was rather smitten by his own handsome features.

'Of course you can come with us,' he said. 'But how are we going to get that key?'

'Follow me, Max,' she answered. 'I know the way.' She led him out of one of the doorways, keeping a careful eye out as they went. Max stayed close behind, too nervous to take in his surroundings and ready to dart for cover at any moment. They wound their way through the maze of rooms inside the temple, Mia glancing constantly around her, alert to the slightest noise or movement. Suddenly, she turned round and hissed, 'Quick, get behind that chair.' He didn't stop to ask why, but did as he was told, hiding himself just in time as he glimpsed swishing blue robes entering the room. He immediately recognised the deep snarling voice.

141

'Get out of my way, you stupid animal.'

Max heard a yelp of pain as the priest's foot shot out and thudded into Mia's body. He bristled angrily, desperate to rush to her aid, but knew this would put an immediate end to their plans, so he bit his tongue and stayed hidden.

'Rami,' bellowed Zorotes.

The bald-headed priest came scuttling into the room.

'Yes, Master?'

'I am retiring for the night. Give me back the key to the cell. I shall be needing it in the morning.' Drawing his lips back he bared his teeth in the manner of a predator about to devour his prey, evidently relishing the prospect of dealing with his prisoners the following day.

Rami reached inside his robes, extracting the key which the high priest snatched off him straightaway. Zorotes pulled the cord over his head and with the key hanging round his neck swept out of the chamber, snarling at Mia once more as he passed. Fortunately this time she managed to remain out of kicking range and waited until Rami had also left the room before coming across to Max's hiding place.

'He's a nasty piece of work, isn't he?' said Max. 'Are you all right, Mia?'

'I'm fine. I've suffered far worse, believe me.'

Max couldn't bear to think of her being hurt, wishing he

could chase after the brutish Zorotes and bite him for his cruelty. He'd been lucky to have only experienced kindness in his own life, apart from annual trips to the vet where they'd stuck needles in him for no apparent reason when he wasn't even ill.

'Now all we've got to do is wait for him to go to sleep,' said Mia. 'It shouldn't take long and we'll know once he's asleep, because his snoring is almost loud enough to bring the temple down around our ears.'

Max hoped that Varna was all right waiting for him outside in the square. It must be dark by now and he was sure she'd be worried. He prayed she hadn't given up and gone home. The two cats remained motionless until the unmistakeable sounds of loud snoring started to echo around the building.

'Right,' said Mia. 'Time to get that key.'

Max's heart was thudding as he followed her out of the room and along a dimly-lit corridor. She stopped outside a doorway. From inside the snoring had reached a deafening level and Max would have liked to put his paws over his ears to drown out the dreadful noise. The two cats crept into the bedchamber where Zorotes lay on an ornate couch, decorated with carved wooden scrolls at either end. A silken sheet covered him up to his middle, but Max could clearly

143

see the key on its cord resting on his chest, rising and falling with each rumbling snore.

'How can we get the key without waking him up?' whispered Max.

'You stay on the floor,' said Mia as she leapt lightly up on to one of the carved wooden scrolls near Zorotes' head. Reaching out a delicate paw she started to push the key slowly off the priest's chest until it dangled by the side of his neck. Suddenly Zorotes gave an extra loud snort and spluttered in his sleep. Mia froze on her perch like a statue, not daring to breathe. Max's heart was in his mouth and he prepared to dive under the bed, but Zorotes just shifted his position a little before relaxing again. Soon the regular sound of his snoring began echoing around the room once more. Mia waited a while and then, extending her trembling paw, she eased the key back to where it had been a few seconds ago. The moment she was satisfied with its position, she leaned across and started nibbling at the leather cord.

'This shouldn't take too long,' she whispered. 'The cord's thin and quite soft. Go over to that chair and fetch the cushion.'

Max looked in the direction of her pointing chin and sure enough a chair stood in the corner of the room, a silken cushion on its seat. He leaped up and nudged it on to the floor.

'Now drag it over here and try to place it where you think the key will fall.'

Max did as she asked, making sure the plump feather-filled pillow was right underneath the exact spot where Mia was gnawing at the cord. Ten agonising minutes went by and each time Zorotes shifted in his sleep or snorted a little louder Mia had to stop what she was doing. She'd almost finished biting through the leather and she stopped, leaning over the side of the bed.

'Get ready, Max. It's about to come loose.' She nibbled a bit more before sitting back on her haunches. 'Now!' she whispered.

The key slipped down the cord and reaching the point where Mia's sharp little teeth had severed the leather it began to fall. Max was terrified in case the key missed the cushion and clattered on to the floor. The noise would definitely wake Zorotes up and Max knew the two of them would be dead cats if that were to happen. He'd positioned it well, however, and the key landed right in the middle with a soft plop. At once Mia jumped lightly down from the bed, displaying the nimble grace of a ballerina.

'Don't just sit there, Max. Pick up the key. We've got to get out of here.'

He didn't need telling twice. Casting one last fearful glance up at the sleeping form of Zorotes he grabbed the key in his mouth and hurried across to the doorway where Mia was already peering out, checking the corridor was empty. 'Let's go,' she said over her shoulder as she slipped out of the room. Max followed and keeping to the shadows they headed swiftly back the way they'd come.

As the two cats ran along the passageway, to their horror, they heard footsteps coming towards them. Max skidded to a halt and, in doing so, bumped into the leg of a table which stood against the wall. On top of the table a large metal jug began to wobble precariously. Horrified, Max's heart almost leaped into his mouth and he froze, not knowing what to do. Mia quickly turned and gave him a shove.

'Hide underneath,' she hissed. Thank goodness the vase didn't fall, but it wobbled some more before righting itself with a loud rattling noise.

'Who's that?' The temple attendant who'd been approaching them stopped in his tracks, peering round the corridor in the gloom. Mia edged out of the shadows and moved towards him, winding herself around his legs and purring. 'Oh it's you, Mia. Are you hunting for mice?'

She mewed quietly in response.

'Go on, best get off to bed and make a little less noise, huh.'

Mia started to walk off and the attendant continued on his way. They made sure he was out of earshot before Max emerged from his hiding place.

'Try not to wake up the whole temple this time,' she said, setting off again.

'Mmmm,' replied Max, which was all he could manage with a mouth full of key.

They arrived at the back door without further incident and emerged into the open air breathing heavily. Max looked frantically around. Where was Varna? Then he spotted her, huddled on a doorstep on the opposite corner of the square. She appeared to be asleep and he gestured to Mia to follow him as he ran across to the step on which Varna was sitting.

'Varna,' he called urgently as he dropped the key in her lap. Her eyes snapped open.

'Max, you've been gone ages. Are you okay?' Then she caught sight of the key. 'Oh well done, you clever cat.' Stretching out a hand to stroke him she spotted Mia who was standing shyly behind Max. 'And who's this?'

'This is Mia,' he explained. 'She helped me get the key. In fact I couldn't have done it without her. She's coming along too because she doesn't want to stay here. Is that all right?'

'Of course,' agreed Varna, turning towards the little chocolate-coloured cat who was regarding her timidly through dazzling emerald eyes. 'Oh you're beautiful, Mia,' she added and, leaning forward, planted a kiss on top of the shiny brown head. 'Thank you for helping us.'

Mia didn't have a clue what the girl was saying, but the gentle tone of her voice and the gesture of affection were things Mia had always longed for and she began to purr.

Varna jumped up from the doorstep. 'Right,' she said. 'Let's go and use this key. Do you need to hide in the basket again, Max, because I'm not sure I'd be able to manage it with both of you inside?'

Max shook his head. 'We should be okay now it's dark. We'll just have to be extra careful.'

# Chapter 19

Varna and the two cats hurried along the dark, deserted street, keeping a watchful eye out for danger and when they arrived at the prison Varna tapped quietly on the door of the cell.

'Jemima, Joe, Charlie, it's us,' she said in a soft voice. 'We've got it.'

Inserting the key in the lock, she quickly turned it and pushed the heavy door open wide to find the relieved children huddled together in the darkness. They were overjoyed to see her and couldn't wait to get out of the cramped, dirty and smelly cell.

'How did ...?' Joe began to speak.

'No time for that right now,' said Varna abruptly. 'We'll explain everything when we get home.'

She thrust her basket into Joe's arms and picking up Max she handed him over to Jemima, before scooping up the smaller cat.

'I'll carry you, Mia,' she said. 'Come on, you lot, we don't want to hang around here. We need to get back home as fast as we can.'

Charlie closed the door of the prison cell behind them and turned the key which was still in the lock, before placing it in his pocket. They set off at a trot down the street, looking all around to make sure no one was around to witness their escape. Jemima held Max tightly against her body, whispering words of praise in his ear whilst they hurried along. Finally, sanctuary was in sight.

Medon was waiting grim-faced just inside the doorway. 'At last. What time do you call this?' he demanded, sounding extremely annoyed, as they all piled into the house.

'I'm sorry, Father,' began Varna, but her voice tailed off as her knees buckled and she started to fall to the floor. He quickly stepped towards his daughter and caught hold of her before she collapsed, helping her across to the bench where she sank down, shaking like a leaf. The enormity of the evening's events had finally caught up with her and delayed shock was setting in. As she sat unable to speak, her teeth chattering, Joe decided they'd better tell Medon everything that had happened. He told him all about Max's kidnapping, Jemima's capture and finally his own and Charlie's abduction. He explained the details of their imprisonment and how Varna had liberated them. By now Varna had recovered enough to add Max's part in the rescue. She was still clinging on to Mia as she recounted her story.

'And this lovely little cat helped him,' she added.

Medon listened to their tale open-mouthed, as if he was finding it too much to take in.

At that moment Aramina came flying down the stairs, uttering a cry of sheer relief. Taking one look at the white-faced, trembling children she rushed towards them, unable to decide which one to hug first.

'But you smell terrible,' she declared, putting her hand over her nose. 'Medon, please go and fetch some water so we can get them cleaned up.' She turned her attention back to the children once more. 'When you've had a wash I'll get you something to eat. Come along, let's get you sorted out.'

The tearful youngsters were so relieved to be back safe and sound they all submitted gratefully to Aramina's cosseting. She tutted at the state they were in, fussing around and comforting them until at last they began to relax, at which point Aramina caught sight of Mia sitting sedately on Varna's knee.

'Ah, Max,' she said. 'You've brought your girlfriend round to meet us. How lovely.'

Everyone laughed, apart from Max who hung his head, squirming with embarrassment.

Later on, after the children had all been washed and fed, Medon and Aramina listened once more to their account of everything that had happened, shaking their heads in disbelief and horror.

'We'll keep you safe and hidden until we leave,' said Medon. 'I promise I won't let those priests get their hands on you again, so don't you worry.'

'I think everyone should get off to bed now,' announced Aramina. 'You must all be worn out and tomorrow's going to be a long day. What shall we do with that little lady?' She gestured to Mia as she spoke.

'Can we keep her, Mother?' asked Varna. 'She needs a home and I've always wanted a cat. Look how beautiful she is.' Varna tickled Mia under the chin, causing the small brown cat to purr with delight.

'All right, we'll talk about that in the morning,' said Aramina.

Mia didn't understand any of what was being discussed, but these people appeared to be friendly and kind, and most importantly she felt safe. Max winked at her as everyone went up to bed and she smiled back at him.

The exhausted, but relieved, youngsters sank on to their straw mattresses which seemed the height of luxury after the time they'd spent in the prison cell and within minutes they were all fast asleep. Jemima clung to Max throughout the night, and for once he didn't complain, quite happy to be squeezed like a teddy bear and snuffling contentedly as he slept.

# Chapter 20

The next day Aramina allowed the children a much needed lie-in while she remained downstairs packing up the family's possessions into giant bundles, using large sheets of material which she secured by tying knots in the corners. She had no intention of going out and leaving the house unprotected with them all asleep upstairs.

Medon, meanwhile, was down at the harbour sorting out last minute arrangements with the other travellers and the merchant who'd agreed to transport some of them. His brother and fellow fishermen wanted to make sure their boats were in good order for the voyage, so they all worked together checking over the sails and oars and applying tar to the wooden planking wherever it was deemed necessary. Finally satisfied the vessels were seaworthy, the men turned their attention to the provisions for the journey and began stacking large earthenware jars containing food and water on the boats in preparation for the following morning's departure. While they helped each other Medon related the previous evening's events concerning the children.

'How awful,' said Delon, Medon's brother. The prospect of something similar happening to his own four offspring filled him with horror. 'So what will happen when the priests realise they've escaped? Won't there be a search party out looking for them?'

'I expect so,' replied Medon. 'But we'll cross that bridge when we come to it.'

'Well, I'm glad we're leaving tomorrow,' said Athos, another fisherman. 'I never trusted that Zorotes, and all the rubbish he spouted about disloyal people abandoning Atlantis was the last straw as far as I'm concerned.'

As the three men sat talking by the boats they were startled by a loud rumble which seemed to come from deep underground, causing the earth to tremble violently beneath their feet. The quake felt stronger than on the previous occasions and the fishermen all regarded each other nervously.

'Are you sure we're doing the right thing?' asked Medon's brother, with a worried expression on his face. 'What if Poseidon *has* decided to punish us? A sea voyage might be a really bad idea.'

'Delon, listen to me. Those earth tremors aren't Poseidon showing us he's angry, but I do think they might

155

signify the start of the disaster. They're getting bigger each day and it can only be a matter of time now. We've made the right decision for our families and we can't leave soon enough in my opinion.'

'I agree with Medon,' said Athos. 'Things can only get worse and, much as I love this place, I'm not sorry we're going.'

Back at the house Aramina and the children ate a quick lunch, while the two cats also enjoyed some special treats in their bowls which had been placed side by side on the floor. After everyone had eaten and cleared away, Aramina asked Varna and Jemima to help sort out the final few items that still needed to be dealt with.

'The packing's almost finished,' sighed Aramina. 'If we've missed anything we'll just have to leave it behind.' She looked around the house a little sadly. This had been her home for so many years and she would miss it more than she was prepared to admit. Still, there was a lot to look forward to and, for the children's sake, she was determined to remain cheerful.

'May I keep the tunic and sandals to remind me of you?' asked Jemima.

'Of course you can,' answered Aramina. 'But I was hoping you might have changed your minds and that you'd

156

be coming with us after all.'

'I'm sorry, Aramina. I wish we could, but we really do need to go home.'

'Oh no,' cried Varna. 'I thought you'd be travelling to Kriti on our boat. I didn't realise you had to go back. I'll miss you so much, all of you.'

'Me too,' replied Jemima. 'You've all been so kind to us and I'm sorry we caused you such a lot of trouble.'

'Nonsense,' declared Aramina. 'You're part of the family now and, don't forget, it's thanks to you we're going to Kriti at all. But I understand why you have to go and I know you want to find your parents.'

'Max and Mia will miss each other too,' said Varna, looking across to where the two cats were indulging in a mutual grooming session. 'I'm so glad I'm allowed to keep Mia. She's gorgeous isn't she? I just hope she doesn't get seasick on the journey. Perhaps you'll be able to come and visit us all in our new home one day?' she added hopefully.

'Perhaps,' answered Jemima, but she knew deep down it was most unlikely. 'At least I've got my drawing as a souvenir too.' She reached for her picture of the Temple of Poseidon. 'Although I'm not sure I particularly want to remember this place after everything those priests did to us.' She showed the sketch to Varna and Aramina.

'Hey, that's brilliant, Jemima,' said Varna as she admired her handiwork.

'Yes, you've got real artistic talent,' agreed Aramina. 'I'm glad my face paint ended up being useful for something.' She laughed.

'I'm sorry I didn't bring the basket and the make-up back,' said Jemima. 'I'm afraid I dropped them in the temple when I was captured. Luckily I still had the picture in my hand, so I tucked it under my belt to keep it safe when they threw me in the cell.'

'Well, I told you I didn't use the make-up any more,' replied Aramina. 'And I'm not short of baskets, so don't worry. Now, I think you two have done enough work for today, so go and find the boys and enjoy yourselves for the rest of the afternoon.'

Jemima and Varna picked up their cats, taking them upstairs to join Joe and Charlie on the roof terrace. They'd been sitting and chatting for about an hour when they heard a loud commotion in the street below. Varna stood up to peer over the parapet. She quickly withdrew her head again.

'It's two of the priests from the temple,' she gasped.

All of the children and both of the cats shrank back on to the mattresses, looking fearfully at one another. None of them wanted to see any of those priests ever again. The shouting down in the street grew louder and Joe decided to risk having a quick peep over the edge. Two men in blue robes were surrounded by a growing group of local inhabitants, including Medon who'd just returned home. The people wielded a variety of implements from brooms to cooking utensils with which they were prodding the nervous-looking men whilst shouting insults at them. All were outraged at the ordeal suffered by the youngsters at the priests' hands.

'We know what you did,' shouted one of them. 'You violated the laws of hospitality by attacking the honoured guests of a respectable family – and they were just children too. You should be ashamed of yourselves. Now, clear off and don't come back.'

Advancing in a menacing manner they jabbed at the priests with their makeshift weapons, forcing them to retreat backwards up the lane. Eventually the two men turned tail and broke into a canter, fleeing back towards the safety of the temple, their robes flapping around their ankles as they ran to escape the mob. Everyone cheered, waving the brooms and assorted sharp implements in the air for good measure, while the children leaned over the wall, surveying the scene in the street below and clapping delightedly.

'Well, that told them,' chortled Joe, as they all rolled

about on the beds, tears of laughter streaming down their faces.

Later in the evening the family enjoyed a final meal in their Atlantean home. Medon, Aramina and their children felt mixed emotions: excitement at the prospect of the new life which lay ahead, nostalgia for the old one they were leaving behind and sadness at the prospect of saying goodbye to their new friends. As for Joe, Jemima and Charlie, they were looking forward to going home, despite being more than a little worried about all the trouble they expected to find themselves in upon their return. On the other hand they too felt rather sad to be leaving the kind family who'd taken them in and, although the past few days had been a bit of a nightmare at times, none of them would ever forget their trip to Atlantis.

# Chapter 21

The following morning everyone was up before dawn, eating a quick breakfast before starting to ferry their bundles and baskets down to the harbourside. Other groups of people had already started to gather near the boats, loading their belongings on board.

On the last trip back to the house Joe pointed to the terracotta sign by the door which showed Medon the fisherman lived there. 'If you're not taking that with you, would you mind if I kept it to remember you all by?'

'Of course you can,' said Medon, rather touched by Joe's request and going round into the back yard he returned carrying a sharp stone which he used to chip the plaque off the wall. He ran his fingers over the surface of the terracotta, before placing the sign in Joe's hand. 'I'll have another one made for our new house when we get to Kriti.'

'Thank you,' replied Joe, curling his fingers around the house sign. 'I promise I'll take good care of this. I'll think of you all and remember Atlantis whenever I look at it.'

Medon smiled as he ruffled Joe's blonde hair with genuine affection.

The sun was rising high in the sky as the last of the cargo was finally loaded on to the boats.

'We should be setting sail now,' said the merchant who'd agreed to help them. People started climbing aboard the vessels, calling encouragement to each other in an attempt to hide their apprehension about a journey into the unknown. At that moment a muffled rumbling sound echoed around the harbour and a violent tremor caused the ground to quake. Even the boats began to rock wildly on the water. Everyone fell silent and stared at one another, fear etched on their faces, wondering if this was the end. However, to everybody's relief the shaking stopped again almost immediately and the loud chattering started up once more as their excitement mounted. Soon all the travellers were ready apart from Medon and his family, who stood beside Joe, Jemima and Charlie on the quayside.

'It's time for us to leave,' said Medon, enfolding them in a warm embrace and patting Max on the head. 'Goodbye to you all. It's been a real pleasure having you as part of our family. I hope you have a safe journey home and that we'll meet again one day, if Poseidon is willing.'

Aramina hugged each of them in turn with tears in her

162

eyes. 'Take care, my dear children.' As she wrapped her arms around Jemima she added in a low voice, 'And I hope you find what you're searching for.'

Jemima nodded, unable to speak because of the huge lump in her throat.

Varna kissed all of them on both cheeks and she clung to Jemima's hands.

'I'll never forget you, Jemima, not ever.'

Max and Mia rubbed noses with each other, saying their own goodbyes.

'You'll have a happy life in Kriti,' said Max, trying to sound cheerful. 'This is a good family and I'm sure they'll be really kind to you.'

'I know, but I'm going to miss you so much, Max,' whispered Mia, a sad expression clouding her beautiful green eyes.

'Me too,' he replied wistfully.

Varna picked the little brown cat up in her arms. 'Come on, Mia. Time to get into your travelling basket.' She lifted her gently inside and Medon stowed it on the boat before helping the rest of his family to embark.

Each vessel pushed away from the quayside and was rowed out of the safety of the harbour while many faces gazed backwards, drinking in the sight of their beloved homeland for one last time. Joe, Jemima and Charlie watched the flotilla of boats begin hoisting their sails as each one headed out to the open sea. Arms held high, they waved with all their might and saw Medon's family waving back at them until they were out of sight. Soon the vessels were no more than dots on the horizon and Jemima stood with tears rolling down her cheeks, as the two boys sniffed loudly, trying to conceal their own emotions.

'Look on the bright side,' said Joe, brushing away an escaped tear. 'We saved them from certain death, didn't we?'

'I do hope they make it to Crete safe and sound,' murmured Jemima. 'I wish we knew for sure.'

'Well, we can return to our own time now,' added Charlie. 'Just think, no one else will ever see Atlantis again after us. Doesn't that seem weird?'

'So, how do we go about finding our way home?' asked Jemima.

'We'd better start by finding the place where we arrived when we first got here,' answered Joe.

The children walked the short distance from the harbour to the beach, with Max trailing miserably at their heels; he was already missing Mia and hoped she'd be all right on the journey. Standing on the sand they gazed around the sea shore, trying to work out the exact spot where they'd first set foot in Atlantis.

'I think it was just about here,' said Jemima, studying their surroundings.

'Okay, so now what?' asked Joe.

Jemima stepped cautiously forward, with one hand on her necklace for good luck and to the boys' amazement she disappeared from sight. One minute she was standing by their side and the next she'd vanished.

'This must be the right place then,' said Charlie. 'So here goes...'

The two boys both stepped forward as Jemima had done, but nothing happened. With Max dawdling absent-mindedly behind, they kept walking further and further towards the sea, but somehow remained stuck on the beach, with no sign of the strange cloud which had transported them to Atlantis in the first place.

'I don't understand,' said Joe. 'Where did Jemima go and why are we still here?'

Meanwhile Jemima had emerged from the swirling mist and found herself back in the house. *Phew*! Everything around her appeared unchanged and she breathed a huge sigh of relief. After a few seconds though, she realised she was alone and that the others hadn't followed her. *Where had they got to*, she wondered? She waited a little while longer and then started to worry, before finally deciding she'd have to return to Atlantis and search for them herself. Reluctantly stepping into the mist once again she found herself back on the beach where she discovered Joe and Charlie stumbling around with their hands held out in front of them as if feeling their way about in the dark.

'What are you two playing at?' she snapped impatiently. 'I thought we were supposed to be going home, but when I arrived you weren't with me.'

'We tried,' said Joe indignantly. 'But nothing happened. Are we stuck here?'

'Well, I didn't have any trouble,' she declared, perplexed. She thought for a moment before realising the problem. 'Ah, I'm the one wearing the necklace, Joe.' The boys stared back at her, both wearing puzzled frowns. 'My gold chain with the key that unlocked the book, remember?' she continued. 'The one Mum and Dad left behind by mistake, which meant they couldn't return.'

The twins had already explained about their parents to Charlie and he now nodded. 'That makes sense,' he said. 'But we can't all be wearing the necklace, so what do we do?'

'Simple,' answered Jemima as she first picked up the glum cat, hoisting him on to her shoulder. 'Hang on tight, Max. Now both of you grab hold of my hands.'

The boys did as she asked and the last thing they all remembered before stepping forwards was hearing a loud rumble as the sand began to shift beneath their feet. The next second they found themselves back in the house, shaking the grains of sand from their shoes.

At once the misty cloud started to grow thin and the image behind them faded until it had vanished altogether, leaving not a single trace of its existence. The children gazed around in amazement. Had it all really happened or had they just imagined everything? The book still lay open on the floor, so Joe placed it carefully inside the wooden box, before returning the chest to the shelf he'd got it from. As he did so, the door opened to reveal Mrs Garland standing there with her hands on her hips. Oh dear, they were for it now.

'I've been calling you for ages,' she said, sounding out of breath. 'Didn't you hear me? I've had to climb all the way up these stairs to fetch you. Well, never mind, dears, come and get your lunch before the food goes cold. You too, Charlie. I presume you're staying.' She looked Jemima up and down, scrutinising her clothes. 'Oh, you're playing at dressing-up – that's nice. What are you supposed to be?'

Jemima glanced down and realised she was still wearing Varna's tunic and sandals. So, the whole thing had been real after all. The three children stared at each other, astonished.

167

Their stay in Atlantis must surely have lasted at least a week, if not longer, and yet time seemed to have stood still here. How strange. Well, at least that meant they weren't going to be in trouble now. What a relief!

# Chapter 22

Joe and Jemima couldn't wait to tell Uncle Richard their news when he came home from work that evening.

'You'll never guess where we've been today,' exclaimed Jemima bouncing up and down, hardly able to contain her excitement. 'Atlantis.' She announced the name in a dramatic voice, expecting him to react with amazement.

'Atlantis?' asked their uncle. 'What's that?' They regarded him as if he'd gone mad. 'Is it a theme park, or a new shopping mall?'

The twins now realised this was going to be more difficult than they'd anticipated and as they danced around him telling him all about their adventure, his only comment was, 'Well, you've both got a vivid imagination, I'll say that for you.'

'Uncle Richard, Atlantis really did exist,' insisted Jemima.

'Yes,' he replied. 'Many historians would like to agree with you on that, but I doubt its existence will ever be proved.'

'I can prove it,' said Jemima and she ran off to fetch her picture. She brought back the piece of material which she presented to her uncle. 'See, here's the Temple of Poseidon.'

He glanced at Jemima's sketch and then did a double take, looking at the drawing more closely. 'What a wonderful picture, Jemima. Did you draw this yourself?'

'I did,' she answered, her voice tinged with pride.

'I expect you copied it from something similar in one of the books in my study, didn't you?' continued her uncle.

'No,' she cried indignantly. 'That's the real Temple of Poseidon which I drew when we were in Atlantis.'

'She's telling the truth,' insisted Joe, a little annoyed at their uncle's reaction. 'We can describe Atlantis and tell you all about some of the people who lived there, like Medon, Aramina, Varna and Mykos...'

'Perhaps later,' muttered Uncle Richard sounding distracted, but as he turned away from them he stared thoughtfully at Jemima's drawing still clutched in his hand. He'd spotted something rather surprising and he needed to go up to his study to investigate it further. If he wasn't mistaken, the script on the pediment of the temple spelled out the name *Poseidon* in Linear B, an ancient Greek form of writing which hadn't been deciphered until the 1950s. Where

170

on earth could Jemima have got that from? Puzzled, he wandered off to his study while Joe and Jemima remained downstairs.

'I said no one would believe us,' said Jemima angrily. 'But I thought at least Uncle Richard might take us a bit more seriously.'

Over dinner that evening, their uncle invited the twins to tell him what they knew of the god Poseidon and Joe repeated the information which Varna had given them during their guided tour of Atlantis. Jemima thought he did look rather astonished when they told him exactly who Poseidon was and why the people of Atlantis considered him to be so important.

Just before Joe and Jemima went up to bed he asked if they'd had any ideas for the following day. He'd promised to take them out somewhere and, the more he thought about it, the more apprehensive he was about what they might come up with.

'We'd like to go to the British Museum,' said Jemima.

Uncle Richard was surprised, although rather delighted by her suggestion.

'Really? Not Legoland or Thorpe Park? Are you sure?'

'Quite sure, thanks,' answered Joe as he winked at Jemima.

171

'Oh, Uncle Richard,' said Jemima over her shoulder as they were leaving the room. 'About Mum and Dad...'

His heart sank. He'd been warned the children might ask difficult questions at times and that he'd have to help them come to terms with their loss. Recently, however, he'd thought they were beginning to cope a little better and seemed to be getting over the worst of their grief.

'... well, they're not dead,' continued Jemima. 'They're just lost and we're going to find them.'

Richard Lancelot groaned inwardly. Nobody had prepared him for anything quite like this and he realised he'd have to get some advice on how to deal with the situation. He smiled fondly at his niece and nephew.

'All right, if that's what you prefer to think for now, but we'll need to talk about it properly when you're ready.' He kissed the twins goodnight and let them go upstairs.

On the landing Joe turned to Jemima, saying, 'Maybe tomorrow we can find something to do with ancient Crete. Wouldn't it be fantastic to discover they all arrived safe and sound?' Jemima agreed with him before disappearing into her bedroom. She was looking forward to sleeping in her own bed and Max curled up next to her as she lay down.

'I do hope Mia's okay,' he murmured in a sad voice. 'I'm so worried about her.'

'I'm sure she'll be fine, Max,' said Jemima as she cuddled him. 'You know Varna will take good care of her.'

In no time at all they'd both fallen into a deep sleep, feeling safe, warm and happy to be home.

# Chapter 23

'So, what would you like to see first of all?' asked Uncle Richard as they entered the foyer of the British Museum.

'Oh, the Greek stuff, please,' answered Joe swiftly.

'Okay, and afterwards we'll do the Romans, followed by the Egyptians. How does that sound to you?'

'Perfect,' said Joe, eager to get going.

Richard was astounded by their apparent enthusiasm. *Perhaps a love of history ran in the family*, he thought, as he turned left towards the Department of Greece and Rome, being thoroughly familiar with the layout of the museum because of his job.

They made straight for the Greek collection and in the first room, which housed artefacts found in the Cyclades islands, Joe and Jemima stopped, transfixed, in front of the glass cases at the sight of so many familiar objects from their stay in Atlantis. The twins moved from display to display, oohing and aahing, while Uncle Richard watched them, totally bemused by their reactions. Jemima studied every single item carefully, reading all the information written on the cards beside each one.

Meanwhile Joe rushed on ahead, keen to find out what else there was. A few minutes later he came flying back, his face flushed with excitement. He'd been in the next room which contained artefacts from the Minoan civilisation.

'Jem, you've got to come and look at this. You won't believe your eyes,' he gasped breathlessly.

Jemima followed him into Room 12 as he ran over to a glass display case, pointing at a small, cracked piece of terracotta bearing the sign of a fish, underneath which were engraved three strange symbols. The label explained the tile formed part of a collection of household items from ancient Crete and Jemima gazed at the object in wonder, a huge smile spreading across her face. Uncle Richard had followed them into the room, curious as to the cause of their excitement.

'What are you two looking at?' he asked, intrigued.

'Those letters say Medon,' explained Joe. 'And he was a fisherman.'

Richard looked at the piece of terracotta and then at the description beside it. The letters did indeed spell Medon, but they were written in Linear B and the card didn't mention the name at all. He stared at the two children in astonishment.

'How on earth did you know that?' he asked.

After a moment's hesitation Joe drew out of his pocket his own plaque which Medon had given him when they'd left the house back in Atlantis and he showed the object to his uncle. Uncle Richard studied Joe's piece of terracotta and then compared the two, before uttering a horrified gasp.

'Have you stolen this, Joe? Give it to me at once and I'll put it straight back. I thought you'd be too sensible to pick up museum exhibits.'

Joe appeared to be on the verge of tears and Jemima immediately leapt to his defence.

'He wouldn't do something like that. He's not a thief and he's not stupid,' she cried. She too felt upset that her uncle could even think such a thing.

Richard stood blinking at them both for a few moments, somewhat bewildered, and he pushed his floppy fringe back off his forehead, as he often did when he was thinking. 'I'm sorry, Joe,' he said, seeing how mortified the two children appeared to be and, with his hands on his hips, he allowed a slow smile to spread across his face. 'Ah, I understand.' He nodded slowly. 'You went into the museum shop when you ran on ahead, didn't you? And this is a replica you've just bought. You had me going for a moment.'

Joe blinked back angry tears, before realising Jemima was shaking her head at him. 'Give up, Joe,' she whispered as she came to stand next to him. 'We knew no one would believe us. Let's keep it as our secret – perhaps it's best that way anyhow.'

Joe nodded, still furious at their uncle's lack of trust in him, but determined to put on a brave face. The rest of the visit passed amiably enough, but Uncle Richard noticed the children seemed to have lost their earlier enthusiasm and he suggested going into the cafe.

'Come on, we'll get some lunch in here before we go home.'

Jemima smiled gratefully at him. Poor Uncle Richard, she thought, he's only doing his best. They ate in awkward silence, but just as they were getting up to leave Joe spoke.

'Thanks, Uncle Richard, it's been interesting, but maybe next time we go out perhaps we could go to somewhere like Alton Towers.' *Ha, that'll teach him*, he thought.

Richard Lancelot's stomach lurched uncomfortably at the prospect, but he nodded gamely, attempting a weak smile.

# Chapter 24

The day after the trip to the British Museum, Uncle Richard had to go to work, so the twins had arranged for Charlie to come round. As soon as he arrived the three of them dashed up to Joe's bedroom, shutting the door to make sure they wouldn't be overheard, before telling him about the terracotta plaque in the museum.

'It was exactly like the one from their house in Atlantis,' explained Joe.

'So they did make it safely to Crete,' said Charlie, beaming. 'Thank goodness.'

The twins also told him about their failure to get Uncle Richard to believe them and the children all agreed from now on they should leave grown-ups out of it altogether.

'My mum still can't understand how I got so sunburned on a rainy day,' grinned Charlie. 'She keeps looking at me really oddly, but I haven't told her anything and I'm not going to either. I think she suspects me of using her fake tan from the bathroom cabinet.'

Jemima and Joe laughed as he told them this. Charlie was right; he did look as if he'd been away on holiday somewhere hot.

'We must keep on searching for Mum and Dad though,' said Jemima earnestly. 'I'm not giving up.'

'Too right,' answered Joe. 'It's brilliant knowing they're still alive, even if they are stuck somewhere in the past – but we've still got the rest of the book to work our way through and we'll just keep going till we find them. At least now we're sure it's safe and that we can always get back here without anyone even noticing we've been missing.'

'As long as we don't forget the necklace,' added Jemima.

'True,' said Joe. 'So, are you in, Charlie?'

'You bet,' agreed Charlie who'd never had such amazing fun in his entire life. During this adventure he'd also discovered a braver side to his character that he hadn't even known existed before and he was keen to see what might happen next time. Putting his hand in his pocket, he squeezed the key to the prison cell in Atlantis, smiling at the memory of their trip.

'And we mustn't forget Max,' said Jemima. 'We'd have ended up stuck in Atlantis without his help.'

'Don't worry,' replied Joe, 'Wherever we go Max goes too. He's one of us now.'

Max, who'd been dozing on the bed, raised his head and gave a solemn nod as Joe said this. 'Yes, you do need someone like me to keep an eye on you and get you out of trouble,' he added rather pompously. 'I can't imagine how much of a mess you might end up in otherwise.'

They all grinned at each other, eager to find out what the next chapter of the book had in store for them.

See you again soon,

Max xxx

# AUTHOR'S NOTE

Since time immemorial scholars, historians and scientists have argued about the lost city of Atlantis. Did it really exist and, if so, where was it situated? Even the ancient Greeks believed the legend to be true, but one thing is for sure: if there ever was such a place, it disappeared off the face of the earth as a result of some sort of natural disaster, never to be seen again.

No evidence has ever been found to support any of the various theories as to where it was, but one of them centres on a particular Greek island in the Cyclades group. In 1700 BC a massive volcanic eruption blew away a major part of Thera (or Santorini as it is also known), leaving the island shaped like a horseshoe with an enormous sea-filled crater at its heart. As a result of the destruction a large bronze age city was totally wiped out. Atlantis, itself, was supposed to have been destroyed by an earthquake, followed by a tidal wave, but the volcanic eruption on Thera would have had an equally devastating effect.

I decided to use this location as the basis for *The Shadow of Atlantis* as it suited my purpose to have events in the story take place in that part of the ancient world. It was also feasible for the family to sail south from there to a new life on the island of Crete. It is here, however, that I have employed a certain amount of artistic licence. If Medon and his family had truly escaped the destruction of Thera, then Crete would have been a rather bad choice. The fallout from the eruption and the subsequent tidal wave is also said to have destroyed much of Crete and its Minoan civilisation.

For those of you who decide to go on and read the next episode in Jemima and Joe's adventures, *The Shadow of the Minotaur*, I am sure you will see why I chose Crete as their destination – and remember ... it is just a story!

# ACKNOWLEDGEMENTS

Thanks to everyone who has helped me along the way.
First and foremost, my husband Simon, my toughest critic
and ruthless editor – I couldn't have done it without you.

A special thank you to my dear friend Clare Allen for her
wonderful drawings of Max.

To all at Mauve Square for their friendship and support, but
especially Shana Silverman for pointing out the Mauve path
when I'd lost my direction and for her constant words of
encouragement. Thanks to my proof-readers, Shana, John
Clewarth and Lisa Williams. And finally, a huge thank you to
the marvellous Annaliese Matheron, our very own
publishing goddess, who helped turn my dreams into reality!

Thanks also to Berni Stevens for her brilliant book cover
design. You are a dream to work with, Berni – I can't wait to
see the next one.

And last but not least, my lovely Bertie, without whom Max
would simply not exist.

# COMING SOON
## THE SECOND BOOK IN THE *SHADOWS* SERIES

# THE SHADOW
# OF THE
# MINOTAUR

Ten-year-old twins Joe and Jemima Lancelot continue the
search for their missing parents who are trapped somewhere
in the past. Together with their friend, Charlie, and their
remarkable talking cat, Max, they are transported back in
time to ancient Crete and the palace of Knossos, where the
fearsome Minotaur resides in its labyrinth, feeding on
human flesh.

Can they help Prince Theseus of Athens overcome the

terrifying monster before it devours them all?

And will the children survive the terrible storm which threatens to wreck their ship as they attempt to flee the island?

www.mauvesquare.com

Printed in Great Britain
by Amazon.co.uk, Ltd.,
Marston Gate.